Sorcha

The MacGregors, Volume 2

Elina Emerald

Published by Elina Emerald, 2021.

SORCHA

First edition. June 12, 2021.

Copyright © 2021 Elina Emerald.

ISBN: 979-8201700652

Written by Elina Emerald.

Table of Contents

To the good ones ...

Chapter 1 – Vengeance

Henderson Keep, Glencoe, Scotland - *6 Months Earlier*

BRAM HENDERSON STOOD in the back of the meeting room at Henderson Keep, his arms folded and his legs spaced apart. He cut a formidable figure given his height and broad shoulders. There was not an inch of fat on his body, just muscle and stealth. Beside him was his younger brother, Niall, and his first cousin, Iain. All of them were of a similar appearance. Each one was impatient to be outdoors, away from the vile stench and filth of their surroundings.

In the front end of the building, close to the central fireplace, sat their laird, Cruim Henderson. He was a boorish man who resembled a hairy mammoth. A round belly from too much ale was his most noticeable feature, along with greasy hair that clung to the sides of his face. The Keep, once sturdy and clean, had since fallen into a slovenly state of disrepair.

Cruim still held power with the old guard, and he ruled with fear and a heavy fist. The way he treated his kin reflected the man he was. His wife, Sarah, sat by Cruim's side, a broken woman with her head downcast from years of subservience, living under the rule of an overbearing man. Two serving women stood behind Sarah, both heavy with child.

It was common knowledge the laird bedded his female servants often. Whether they were willing was doubtful. He had enough illegitimate children across the length of Alba to form his own clan.

Bram had gone to great lengths to keep his sister Willa and his cousin Tyra away from Cruim's line of sight.

Cruim stood to address the men. "I have called you all here because 'tis time we allied with the Campbells," he said in a gravelly voice.

There were murmurings and angry grunts amongst the men.

"What happened to an alliance with the MacDonalds?" Bram asked.

The Hendersons were a sept of Clan MacDonald; it seemed strange that Cruim would side with the Campbells instead.

Cruim replied, "The Campbells are stronger, and if we are to become conquerors, we must align with those who can bring more benefit to us."

"Why do we need this alliance?" Niall shouted.

"Because the MacGregors are raiding our lands again," Cruim replied. "We need a mighty clan on our side so we can stand against them."

"We still have no proof it was the MacGregors," Iain interjected.

"My son Grant found a scrap of their plaid in the thickets after a raid." Cruim held up the torn piece of material bearing the MacGregor colors.

"'Tis still not a sound enough reason to ally with the Campbells," Bram argued.

Several clansmen nodded in agreement.

Cruim turned red in the face, and then he thumped his swollen fist on the table, startling them all. "I am laird here, and I decide what course we take!" he growled, spittle bursting from his mouth. "Anyone who wants to challenge me can do so right now." Cruim clenched his fists as his guardsmen put their hands to their swords.

The room went quiet. Several clansmen, including Niall and Iain, glanced at Bram. Bram shook his head as a subtle gesture for them to remain silent.

Cruim scowled and said, "In a sennight's time, we will ally with the Campbells, and you'll see the right of it when the MacGregors come raiding again."

Three Days Later

BRAM CAME AWAKE WITH a jolt as Niall stood over his bed, shaking him.

"Bram, Willa is gone," Niall said, his voice filled with panic.

Bram was on his feet in an instant. In a quick succession of movements, he donned his plaid and untanned shoes.

"What has happened?" Bram growled as he reached for his broadsword and targe.

"The MacGregors are raiding by the river. I went to check the cottages, but Willa is not there."

Bram cursed, then ran for the door of their longhouse. His movements roused the family as his mother, niece, and nephews appeared from their rooms, their worried faces illumined by the fireplace.

"Where do you go?" his mother, Fia, asked.

"To find Willa. There is a raiding party. Bar the door when we leave and remain inside."

"Aye, but be careful, Bram," Fia said.

He nodded, then stepped out into the darkness and ran. Bram's heart pounded with fear for his sister Willa. He prayed she did not fall victim to the raiding party.

By the moon's light, with frost burning through his lungs, Bram kept pace with Niall and Iain. They were running several yards apart through the dense woodlands. His eyes trained straight ahead. His breathing was steady as he ran with ease along the banks of the River Coe. Bram held a sword in one hand and a targe in the other. He and his clansmen had hunted this way for years, but this time the game they hunted was human.

Bram saw something in the distance that made his blood run cold. A man wearing a plaid bearing the MacGregor colors was shouting at Willa. Bram could not quite make out his face, but before he reached them, the man pushed Willa into the rapids. Bram heard Willa's piercing scream and a loud splash as she hit the water.

He roared, "No!" He sprinted towards the river's edge while the MacGregor took flight.

Torn between giving chase and saving his sister, Bram instantly dived in after her. But the fast-moving current and murky waters made it difficult to reach her. He could just make out Iain giving chase after Willa's attacker while Niall tumbled down a ravine, trying to reach her from the riverbank.

Willa's body bobbed in the water like driftwood as the current carried her further away.

"Willa, take my hand!" Bram yelled, coming within a hand's length of her. He was battling against the current and losing. Willa would not even reach for him.

"Willa! Damn you, take my hand!" Bram shouted again, desperate to grab her arm.

Before his eyes, Willa sank underwater and disappeared.

He and Niall tried desperately to find her, but to no avail. The current was too strong, and the darkness hampered their view.

The following morning at first light, Bram and his men searched the riverbank, to no avail. They had to face the reality that Willa was dead. Murdered by a MacGregor. Bram knew Cruim was right. An alliance with the Campbells was the only way to defeat the bastards.

Bram and Iain were just preparing to return home after another futile search when he saw a flicker of the MacGregor plaid among the tree line. Someone was watching them from the hillside. The spy turned to flee when Iain took off in pursuit on foot. Bram mounted his horse and followed. Hendersons were excellent runners, but as horsemen, they were exceptional.

Bram urged his horse into a faster gallop, giving chase. He carefully weaved through the trees as horse and rider became one. He was closing the distance. Bram was mere yards away from the assailant when he heard a great commotion nearby. The sound of a body landing hard against the ground with a thud reverberated through the forest.

He whipped his head to the side and saw Iain on the ground with an arrow pierced through his shoulder. Bram barely had time to duck when a volley of arrows came flying his way. There was an archer in the trees.

Bram grabbed the targe that was fastened to his saddle and shielded himself. He veered his horse towards Iain. He was not prepared to lose any more kin. Bram reached down and hauled Iain onto his horse without stopping. He aimed to move out of the reach of the longbow. When he surveyed the ridge, both men had disappeared.

Bram roared, "Damn you MacGregor scum!"

Raucous laughter was the only response as the sound of voices drifted further away in the distance.

"Sorry cousin, I was not looking," Iain said; remorse tinged his voice.

"Dinnae fash yourself, 'tis the MacGregor bastards who are to blame for all that has befallen our clan."

Bram's Longhouse, Henderson Land, Glencoe

THE HOUSEHOLD WAS IN mourning. Bram's mother, Fia, had taken to her bed in a state of shock. Their cousin Tyra was helping with the younger siblings who were bereft, losing their beloved aunt, Willa.

Into this grief-stricken home, Bram helped Iain into the house with one arm under his shoulder.

Tyra immediately stood to assist him while the younger siblings looked on in surprise. "What the devil happened now?" she whispered.

"MacGregors," Bram replied.

Tyra was their makeshift clan healer. Since they were children, Tyra had mended their cuts and scrapes. With deft fingers and Bram's help, she staunched the bleeding and dressed the wound.

"Why are the MacGregors determined to destroy us?" Tyra asked in a voice that held a contralto-like tone with a soft lilt.

"I dinnae ken why, but it just makes no sense," Iain said.

"I will speak to the laird," Bram replied. "Willa's death cannot go unpunished. We have no choice but to ally with the Campbells."

Tyra said, "No, we will end up worse off for it. Bram, 'tis time you took your rightful place as our leader and talked to the MacDonalds—"

"Wheesht, dinnae speak such words, Tyra. We canna go against our laird," Bram replied.

"Bram is right, Tyra, 'tis thoughts like that can get you killed if Cruim hears you," Fia said as she approached the table to join them. Her eyes were etched with grief. "Dinnae do anything brash. I have already lost so much. I cannot bear to lose either of you."

Henderson Keep, Glencoe - Clan Meeting

"GIVEN THE LATEST MURDER and raid, I have sent word to the Campbells that we will be agreeable to an alliance so we can rid ourselves of the MacGregors," Cruim said.

Bram simply nodded his head.

"I say we strike back and pillage the MacGregor's stocks for a change," Grant said.

There was a quiet murmuring in the room.

"'Tis a novel suggestion, son," Cruim praised Grant.

"When do you suggest we do this?" Bram asked.

"We strike during Christmas."

"With respect, Chieftain, the weather is the worst during that time. We could freeze to death raiding stores in the bitter cold," Iain said.

"When people are cold, they let their guards down," Cruim replied.

"I agree with Iain, I dinnae think 'tis a good time to go raiding," Bram said.

Cruim roared, "The MacGregors declared war when they murdered Willa, or have you already forgotten?"

Bram shook his head.

"Good, then you will lead a raiding party on Christmas Day. I am not asking you, Bram; I am ordering you as your laird to see to it."

Bram clenched his jaw and replied, "Aye. It shall be done."

"I will go as well," Iain piped in.

"Aye, me too," Niall said.

Cruim replied, "Good. I will send Grant to go with you as well."

Bram could feel the tension around the room at the mention of Grant. No one liked him or trusted him because he was Cruim's son. He was also cunning and lazy, but they had no choice.

Cruim said, "Make sure you dinnae come back empty-handed."

When they were out of earshot, Iain approached Bram outside and quietly murmured, "Grant will spy for his da, be careful what you say."

"Aye, that is why I will keep him close," Bram replied.

1046 Christmas, MacGregor Land, Glenorchy, Scotland

BRAM OBSERVED FROM a safe distance the movements of the MacGregor Clan. He had been keeping a close eye, waiting for the right moment to strike. It had been a harsh winter, with poachers and dwindling food supplies.

The raid was quick and efficient. They split up into two groups. Bram kept watch over Grant while Niall and Iain raided a different location. The MacGregors were busy celebrating Christmas with extended clans, oblivious that their stocks were being ransacked.

The MacGregor stores were better stocked than Bram had dared hope. Salted fish, dried venison, two barrels of mead. It was enough to see his people through to the thaw if they were careful. He slung the last sack over Grant's shoulder and his own, and they struck out across the white field toward the treeline where their horses were tethered, boots crunching through crust-iced snow, wind cutting hard enough to sting any bare skin it found.

They were halfway to the trees when he heard it. A voice, thin and cracked, barely carrying over the wind.

"Help."

Grant kept walking. "Leave it."

Bram stopped.

"Bram." Grant's voice had an edge now. "We've got what we came for. Dinnae be a fool."

He followed the sound instead of his sense, picking his way toward an old stone well half-collapsed at its lip, snow drifted thick around the rim. Bram leaned over the edge and saw, far below in the dark, a small, huddled shape.

"This is not part of the plan," Grant hissed, catching up to him. "What the bloody hell do you think you're doing?"

"We canna leave him here. He will die."

"What do we care about a MacGregor? Let the runt die."

Bram was already shrugging the sack off his shoulder, dropping it into the snow at his feet. Whatever fury still burned in him over Willa, it had no place here, not against a mere lad who'd done nothing but get himself stuck down a well on the coldest night of the year. He would spend his rage on Beiste MacGregor and no one else.

He unslung the rope coiled at his hip. "He's just a bairn." He tied it off against the old well post and tested his weight against it. "Lower the rope. I am going down to get him."

"Dinnae be a fool, leave him or you will get us all killed before we've even begun."

Bram turned and fixed Grant with a steely glare. "Shut your mouth and hold the damned rope."

Grant swore under his breath but took hold, setting his own sack down beside Bram's.

Bram went over the edge.

The descent was slow, the stone slick with ice, his hands burning before he was halfway down. Below him, the boy had gone quiet — too quiet. The child looked no older than seven or eight, lips gone faintly blue, shivering so hard his teeth clattered.

The boy's eyes fluttered open. "Please, mister, dinnae leave me here."

"I willna leave you, lad." Bram finally reached him. He pulled the wool plaid from his own shoulders and wrapped it tight around the boy's small frame, then gathered him up against his chest. He gave the rope two hard tugs.

Grant hauled from above, and Bram climbed with one arm, the boy clutched in the other, his shoulders screaming by the time he hooked an elbow over the rim and rolled them both onto the snow.

The boy's eyes were already drooping shut.

"Dinnae sleep, lad. Stay alert." Bram shook him gently, and the boy's eyes blinked open again, glassy and unfocused.

Grant stood over them both, scowling down at the bundle in Bram's arms. "He's burning up with fever. We need a healer."

"And how do you suggest we manage that?" Grant scoffed, folding his arms. "The only healer worth a damn is the Beiste's wife. Do ye want us to march into the Keep and ask for her?"

Bram said nothing for a moment, his mind working before he found his solution.

"There is another healer," Bram replied. "An old crone who lives apart from the rest, near the eastern ridge. I have seen her gathering herbs more than once and marked where she dwells." He rose to his full height, the boy held fast against his chest, his cloak snapping out behind him in the wind. "We take him there."

Grant didn't argue further. He hefted both sacks of stolen stores over his own shoulders, muttering the whole while, and stalked off toward where they'd left the horses tethered at the edge of the trees.

Bram lifted the boy higher against his shoulder and strode after him, broad and unhurried despite the urgency in his step, the wind tearing at his plaid and cloak the whole way.

At the horses, Grant lashed both sacks behind his saddle, freeing Bram to mount with the boy held secure against his chest, one arm locked around the small body, the reins gathered in his other hand. They rode hard for the eastern ridge, the boy's fevered breath warm and uneven against his neck.

THE COTTAGE SAT LOW and crooked against the hillside, smoke curling thin from its chimney, swallowed almost as soon as it rose by the wind. Bram swung down from his horse, the boy still cradled against him, and left Grant to settle both mounts and the stolen sacks at the edge of the clearing.

He stood on the threshold, cloak billowing wide around his frame, and knocked once with his boot since both his hands were full.

The door opened, and a woman appeared in the gap — grey-haired, weathered, her eyes a strange, washed grey-white that caught the firelight behind her.

"Och, so ye have finally decided to reveal yourself, Highlander," she said.

It unsettled him more than he cared to admit, and Bram did not unsettle easily. He drew himself up taller. "I dinnae have time for riddles, old woman. The bairn needs help; he is half frozen."

She studied the bundle in his arms and her manner shifted at once, and she stepped back to let him pass.

Between them they stripped the boy's wet clothes and laid him on a cot by the fire, rugged in dry blankets while Morag fed the flames higher. Bram stood by, watching the boy's chest rise and fall in shallow, rattling breaths.

When he was satisfied there was nothing more he could do, he turned to leave.

Morag's hand closed around his arm with surprising strength.

"You made the right decision today, Highlander. Your good deed will come full circle."

He pulled his arm free, his jaw tight. "I dinnae need your predictions, witch. I have wasted precious time already."

"Tsk. So impatient." Morag was already reaching into the folds of her shawl, drawing out something small wrapped in cloth. She held it out to him. "Ye best prepare for what is coming."

Bram stared at the little package without taking it. "What is this for?"

"'Tis the difference between life and death."

He clenched his jaw, snatched it from her palm, and shoved it into his pocket. He gave her a short, hard nod and stepped back out into the bitter night.

THE WIND HAD PICKED up since they'd gone inside, sweeping hard down off the ridge and driving loose snow sideways across the path. Bram pulled his cloak tighter at the throat and started toward the treeline, where Grant stood waiting with both horses, stamping his feet against the cold.

He had taken no more than a few strides when movement on the path caught his eye — a figure running hard up the slope, breath ragged and visible in sharp clouds against the dark.

Bram stopped.

Her hood fell back as she ran, and gold hair tore loose in the wind around a face that struck the breath clean out of him. She was flushed from the cold and the running, eyes blazing, already shaping words before she'd even reached him. Their eyes locked across the short distance between them, and something in his chest twisted.

Bram inhaled sharply.

Then she shocked him when she rapidly pulled a bow from her shoulder, nocked an arrow with hands that didn't shake despite the cold, and leveled it at his chest.

"Who are you and where is Jordie?" she demanded.

"If you mean the bairn I found in the snow, he is inside the cottage, lass."

"Then what are you doing here?" Her tone was sharp and unyielding.

"'Tis none of your concern." Bram held his ground and let his eyes move over her — the fine weave beneath the plain cloak thrown over it, the golden hair, the stories he'd heard about her talent with a bow. He knew exactly whose blood ran in her veins, and that was enough.

She held the arrow steady, but in the distance behind her, voices carried through the trees — men's voices, drawing closer, calling her name.

Grant's growl carried across the clearing. "We have to go now!"

The sound startled her, and her aim wavered as she registered for the first time that there was a second man at the treeline. She swung her arrow toward Grant instead, and that single heartbeat of distraction was all Bram needed.

He closed the distance before she could correct her aim, caught her wrist, and twisted the bow free of her grip.

"Sorry, beauty," Bram said, low, "but I dinnae have time today. We shall meet again and become better acquainted."

Behind her, the voices were closer now. Bram didn't wait. He threw her weapons aside, caught the edge of her hood, and yanked it down hard over her eyes, spinning her by the shoulder and shoving her into a snowbank.

Bram was already running before she hit the ground.

He swung up onto his horse beside Grant, who was already mounted and kicking his own horse into motion, the stolen sacks still lashed behind his saddle. They tore down the path and into the cover of the trees.

It wasn't until they'd put real distance between themselves and MacGregor land — until the wind had scoured the heat from his blood and left something colder and clearer in its place — that the thought arrived, fully formed.

Bram hadn't simply stumbled upon a beautiful stranger in the snow.

He'd stumbled upon Beiste MacGregor's sheltered sister.

A woman like that — sister to the Beast himself — was worth more to Bram than every blade his clan could muster.

He urged his horse faster into the dark, the shape of his vengeance already turning over in his mind, gold hair and a blazing, fearless glare burned into the center of it.

Willa's death would not go unanswered. And Bram had just found exactly how he meant to answer it.

The Longhouse, Glencoe, Scotland

"THE BEAST HAS A SISTER," Bram said.

His men were quiet.

"How old?" Iain asked.

"She's a woman grown. Unwed, no betrothal."

"Why was she not sent away to the abbey if she is unwed?" Iain asked.

"The villagers say she could not speak when she was a bairn. The Beast's wife tutored her in the Keep, and she has remained there ever since," Bram replied. "They are verra protective of her."

"No doubt they will pawn her off soon to make some alliance of Macbeth's choosing," Niall snorted.

"Aye, and ye ken what that means, brother?" Bram asked.

There was silence as it suddenly dawned on them.

"It means she is the most valuable person to capture," Iain replied.

The men grinned. Then Bram turned to his cousin Tyra and said, "I need you to make friends with Sorcha MacGregor."

Chapter 2 – Present Day

1047 MacGregor Land, Glenorchy, Scotland

SORCHA BRIMMED WITH excitement as she made her way to the abandoned cottage with a pouch filled with goods. She had arranged to meet Tyra there, and Tyra's friends would escort them to the village dance. Sorcha felt beautiful wearing the pale blue kirtle and Tyra's clan's airisaidh. It was blue and green with white squares and faint yellow cross stars.

Sorcha's hair hung loosely around her shoulders. She preferred the darker brown color she had dyed it to her natural blonde locks. Sorcha looked and felt feminine, as it was one of the few times she did not wear trews.

She was about to knock on the door when Tyra opened it and squealed with excitement.

"Dinnae dally, come inside," Tyra said. A hint of amusement sparkled in her eyes.

Tyra had chestnut-colored hair. She was very comely with hazel eyes and dimples that appeared when she smiled. Tyra was fiercely independent and fascinated Sorcha with her knowledge of the world. Sorcha also knew that Tyra turned heads. Lachlan, one of Beiste's guardsmen, could not keep his eyes off her whenever he was guarding Sorcha. Tyra insisted there was nothing to it, just mere flirtation.

"Why are ye not dressed yet?" Sorcha asked, noticing that Tyra was in trews and a tunic.

"Patience, my dearest friend, it will not take long for me to change. But first, let me pour us something strong to drink... it will make our cheeks rosy so we can attract some braw men."

Sorcha laughed and took a seat as Tyra bustled around the room, fixing them refreshments.

"Tyra, who are your friends who will escort us?"

"'Tis just some clansmen from the burgh. They are passing through."

"Will they be staying for the dance?" Sorcha asked.

"Aye, although I dare say they will have women fawning all over them so they will not be in our way."

Tyra returned with two cups of mead. "Here, let's toast to a wild night of dancing and men!" She winked and giggled.

Sorcha grinned and raised her glass, saying, "Aye, to braw, handsome men!"

Tyra skulled her drink, and Sorcha did the same.

"Right, now, I shall get dressed before my friends arrive. And Sorcha... you look truly bonnie tonight. I doubt any man will take their eyes off you," Tyra said with a sad smile.

Sorcha felt the mead hit her and warm her belly. She was happy to escape the stifling guardsmen and looked forward to the dance. This was her one night of freedom, and she was going to enjoy it for all it was worth.

She observed Tyra move about the room and started feeling a little drowsy. Sorcha stifled a yawn and shook herself awake. "Oh, dear, I think I drank that mead too fast. It has gone directly to my head," she said.

"Aye, it does that sometimes. Dinnae worry, you will feel better soon. Just think of your first kiss, and you will have the energy to dance all night," Tyra replied.

Sorcha smiled at the pleasant thoughts. She heard a knock at the door, as Tyra said, "Come in."

Sorcha stood to greet the newcomers, and it brought on a dizzy spell. She grabbed the back of the chair to steady herself when the door slowly opened. A large-hooded man stood in the doorway.

A prickly feeling shot up her spine. Something told her she was in danger. She tried to focus, but her mind felt fragmented and her body lethargic. Sorcha glanced at the cup, then she glared at Tyra.

"What have you done to me?" Sorcha asked, betrayal lacing her tone.

"I am sorry, Sorcha, truly I am," Tyra replied guiltily. "But we have no choice."

Sorcha grabbed the bread knife off the table, but her grip was weak, and it slipped through her fingers.

The man crossed over the threshold and moved closer. When he removed his hood, Sorcha came face to face with the Highlander who saved Jordie in the snowstorm.

"Hello, lass, 'tis time we got better acquainted," he said.

"Stay away!" Sorcha cried out and tried to move backward but was unsteady on her feet.

He continued to stalk her.

"What do you want?" she asked in a fearful voice.

"You, Sorcha. I want you," he replied.

The last thing Sorcha glimpsed was the Highlander reaching for her before she blacked out.

BRAM CAUGHT SORCHA just in time and lifted her into his arms just as her body went limp.

He instinctively held her tighter against his chest. He pondered how perfectly she fit against him. Then he shook his head. What the hell was wrong with him? She was the enemy.

With a worried frown, he asked Tyra, "How much did you give her? She is out cold."

"Dinnae worry, 'tis just enough for her to remain quiet until we are far away from here."

Tyra was packing up her things. She also picked up Sorcha's bag and doused the fire.

"Are you sure it was necessary to drug her?" Niall asked as he entered the cottage.

"Aye, if you only ken how strong she is when she is in a fighting mood, you'll both thank me later," Tyra replied.

"I doubt someone her size can be much trouble," Niall said.

"You are wrong, cousin. Her guard was down because she trusted me. Any other time and she would have sliced your neck with that blade."

"But she is too bonnie to be a fighter," Niall replied.

"Dinnae call her bonnie! Remember, she is our enemy," Bram growled, feeling possessive towards her. It did not help matters that Sorcha wore the Henderson colors, which he liked seeing on her.

"She is not like other women, Niall. She is rebellious and headstrong," Tyra said.

"Well, that does not bode well for her. Cruim will crush her defiance," Niall replied.

"Aye, if she was not a MacGregor, I could almost feel sorry for her," Bram said before ordering them to ride.

TEN MINUTES LATER, the three of them were on horseback. Bram rode in front, guarding the others.

Niall rode in the middle with Sorcha in his lap, and Tyra brought up the rear. They were just leaving MacGregor land when they startled a group of children playing in the woods.

"Damn!" Bram cursed. "What the devil are they doing here?"

"That's my aunt!" one lass shouted.

Not long after, he heard Niall cry out in pain, "Bram!"

Bram turned and noticed Niall had an arrow lodged in his thigh and was barely keeping hold of Sorcha.

He turned his horse around, galloped towards his brother, and roared at the children as they fled.

Tyra was by Niall's side. She quickly broke off the arrow shaft and fletching which was protruding from the wound while Bram transferred Sorcha into his arms.

"Can ye ride, brother?" Bram yelled.

"Aye," Niall nodded as he winced in pain.

"Then we best move before the bairns bring the wrath of the Beast upon us," Bram said. He wrapped Sorcha in his plaid, settled her close against his chest, then urged his horse forward. "Dinnae stop for any reason," he yelled, as the three of them rode as fast as they could.

The First Escape

IT WAS SEVERAL HOURS later when Sorcha roused from her sleep. The first thing she was aware of was being in someone's arms. She could smell woodlands and leather and welcomed the warmth. She snuggled closer before realizing she was moving. It all flooded back to her that she was in danger.

Her body stiffened, and the arms around her tightened.

A rumbling voice spoke against her ear, "Steady, lass, I mean you no harm."

She leaned forward, but her captor's arms were like iron manacles, and he kept her in place.

Her wrists were bound, and they had placed a gag around her mouth.

She immediately took in her surroundings. It was nighttime, and they were on horseback and riding fast. Whoever they were, they were excellent horsemen to navigate their way by moonlight.

She saw another horseman and Tyra riding close behind.

Sorcha needed to escape, and under the cover of darkness was the best chance she had. She knew a maneuver Brodie had shown her, it was a way of rolling off a horse without causing too much damage. Despite her hands being bound, she could still pull it off if she could just get the arms holding her to loosen a little.

"Whatever it is you are thinking, 'tis best you cease, or you could get yourself killed," Bram said.

His warning startled her. It was as if he could read her mind.

Sorcha hesitated only a moment. Then she lifted her arms straight up in the air, then brought her elbows down hard against his, nudging them away from her body, causing him to loosen his grip. She flung her head backward, knocking him hard on the chin.

"Ouch," he growled as his head snapped back and he almost fell off the horse.

That was all Sorcha needed. She went limp and slid downward.

"Bloody hell!" Bram yelled as he tried to pull up her dead weight with one hand while holding the reins with his other. He could not get a decent grip.

Sorcha had timed it well. Her feet hit the ground, and she tucked and rolled out of the way of the horse's hooves. She landed hard on her hip, but adrenaline was pumping and she was already on her feet and rushing into the darkened forest.

She could hear the Highlander cursing and his company shouting as they slowed their horses.

Sorcha did not look back. She knew she had a small window of time to put as much distance between them, and she ran.

BRAM CURSED AS HE DISMOUNTED. "Stay alert, I'll be back," he yelled at Tyra and Niall before he sprinted after his captive. His heart had lodged in his throat when he thought Sorcha was about to be trampled to death. He breathed a sigh of relief when he saw her scoot off into the woods. If he wasn't so furious that she had endangered her life, he might even be a little in awe of the maneuver.

Bram saw the movement of foliage up ahead and knew the direction she was traveling. She was moving faster than any lass he had ever met before. He realized then he had underestimated her. It would pay to heed Tyra's words. Sorcha MacGregor was no ordinary lass. Even running with minimal visibility and at a disadvantage, she was swift on her feet.

Still, the thrill of the chase invigorated Bram. He would very much enjoy chasing her down. She brought out the primal instinct in him. He had known it the first time he clapped eyes on her. It was like thousands of fireflies lit up the night sky when she had the nerve to point an arrow at him. Even now, she still did not fail to surprise him. Bram only hoped he found her soon because as dangerous as *he* was, the woods held far more sinister creatures, mostly two-legged ones.

Avenging Angel

SORCHA'S LUNGS WERE burning, but she would not stop. She weaved her way through trees in a zigzag motion so someone tracking her would have difficulty reading her movements. She would figure everything else out later, as long as she maintained her distance from her captors. She was so focused on looking backward she failed to notice the three men ahead until she crashed headlong into one of them.

He immediately banded his arms around her and said, "Weil, what do we have here then, lads? A bonnie wee sprite."

Sorcha knew they were mercenaries of the worst kind. With her hands bound, she was at a disadvantage, but she still tried to leverage her weight against his. She bent low, reached down and grabbed his ankle, stood and pulled hard. Her attacker lost his footing and fell back onto the ground. She turned to run, but two others grabbed her and forced her onto the ground. One held down her arms while the other captured her legs. All her moves were futile against two powerful men. But she still fought like a wildcat to break free, with no success. Sorcha stopped before she tired herself out. She needed to conserve her energy and take stock of the situation.

She shuddered when the one she had pushed to the ground rose above her. His eyes raked over her with a look of pure lust. She realized then she was a lone woman in the forest at night, at their mercy.

He gave her a wicked smile, then he began undoing his trews. Sorcha screamed through the gag and tried to kick at him, but she was pinned down firmly.

"Och, save yer screaming, lass, for when my shaft is rutting hard inside you." He guffawed.

Sorcha tried to move her hands, but the second man held her steadfastly. He tore the front of her dress open and squeezed her bare breast.

"I want to go next when ye're finished with her," he said.

The third man just chuckled as he pushed her tunic higher to expose her thigh. Sorcha felt the cold air hit her flesh. A shadow hovered above her as the first man kneeled between her legs, pulling his trews further down.

Sorcha struggled harder but could not break free, and she knew what was about to happen. She resolved to fight until the end. She closed her eyes and mentally prepared herself to survive no matter the cost, even as tears trickled down her face at the futility of her predicament. She blocked out the sound of their cackling and the feel of their rough hands groping her, and she braced for the inevitable.

Then she heard something. It was running footsteps, a rustling noise, and an almighty roar like a lion. What followed was a whooshing sound. She opened her eyes in time to see the head of the man who was kneeling over her roll a few yards away. His headless body slumped backward and hit the ground.

Then the one holding her legs screamed in pain and released her as a sharp sword burst through his chest from behind. She saw the blade retreat and watched as a shod foot kicked his body away from her. It was then a gigantic figure blocked the moonlight, and Sorcha stared straight up into the eyes of her Highland captor. Like an avenging angel, his sword dripped with blood, and he was livid.

The man fondling her breast had a wide-eyed look of fright just before the Highlander plunged his blade into the man's chest. He made gurgling sounds, then fell down dead.

The Highlander wiped his blade on the man's clothes, then sheathed his sword.

Sorcha was trembling. She sat up and pulled the front of her kirtle together with her bound hands, as she tried to cover her breast. She attempted to stand, but there was no need because she was lifted straight into the arms of the Highlander.

He did not speak a word; he just clenched his jaw, held her tighter to his chest, stepped over the dead bodies, and walked back the way he came.

The flight response left Sorcha, and understanding the gravity of what she had just escaped, she buried her face into her captor's neck and wept like a baby. She felt his lips brush against her forehead, and she clung to him tighter, grateful that he had saved her.

BRAM WANTED TO KILL every one of those men again. He was furious about what they had intended to do. As he held his weeping captive in his arms, he made a promise that, enemy or not, he would guard her with his life.

When he rejoined the others, he freed her hands, undid her gag, and helped her retie the front of her garment. She was still in a state of shock; she let him do it. Bram doubted she would run away again so soon.

Tyra and Niall sported pitying expressions and helped where they could. They also observed Bram and remained quiet. They had never seen him act this way towards anyone before.

Bram lifted Sorcha onto his horse, jumped up behind her, wrapped his plaid around her, and held her tight. Then he ordered them to ride.

The Bothy

SORCHA AND HER CAPTORS stopped for the night in a small bothy by a stream. This gave them time to rest the horses, eat a light repast, and get some sleep. They gave her some privacy to relieve herself behind a tree, and Tyra gave her a washcloth and change of clothes to freshen up in the nearby stream. Sorcha still did not know why they had taken her captive, and she refused to speak or make eye contact with Tyra. She felt betrayed so deeply and adrift without her clan. At least she had learned their names. Her captor was Bram, his brother was Niall, and they were Tyra's cousins. Bram was currently keeping watch over her as she washed and changed clothes. He had his back partially to her as he scanned the woods.

When she was done, he clasped her hand in his and walked her back to the bothy. He then tied her hands and ankles so she could not escape, and then the three of them took turns seeing to their own needs. When Bram returned, his hair was wet as he had bathed in the stream.

When they were all settled, they shared a light meal. Sorcha had her back against the wall, and she was chewing on some dried meat and an oatcake. She needed energy and sustenance, and she was starving, having not eaten anything all day. At some point, she resolved she would try to escape, but now was not the time. She needed to regroup and re-plan when she had more weapons. She drank only clear water and sniffed it first.

"Why have you taken me captive?" she asked.

They were silent until Bram replied, "As payback for what your clan has done to mine."

Sorcha pricked up her ears. "And what have we done?"

"The MacGregors raid our lands regularly," Bram replied.

Sorcha snorted. "Every clan goes raiding once in a while. 'Tis no reason to take me captive!"

Niall then said, "Aye, but does every clan murder your sister?"

Sorcha stilled. "What do you mean?" she asked.

"Your clansmen raided our stores, left us with nearly nothing to eat. Then one of them murdered our sister."

"No! That canna be. We are many things, but we are not murderers. My brother Beiste would not stand for it—"

"Your brother approves of the raids. How else does your clan have so much food each winter?" Bram asked.

"We have food because everyone works and does their share. There must be some mistake." Sorcha was vehement in the defense of her kin. "No, you are wrong. Beiste is not like that; my brother is a fair man and he would never—"

Niall scoffed, "Your brother, the Beast of the Highlands, is a fair man? Surely you jest."

"'Tis true, Sorcha, it was a MacGregor who killed their sister Willa. I kenned it also. A MacGregor took her captive, and he murdered her," Tyra replied.

Sorcha just shook her head. "This makes no sense. There must be some other reason. If you just let me speak to Beiste and my kin, they will ken the truth. If not, then my sisters will ken what is happening; my brothers confide in their wives."

"Men have a way of showing a different nature to their wives than the rest of the world," Bram replied. "I saw with my own eyes a

MacGregor push my sister into a raging river, knowing full well she would drown."

Sorcha was shocked. She kept shaking her head. "I am sorry for your sister, truly I am. But if this is true, then it is not because of my brother. He does not condone the murder of women."

Bram was pensive as he contemplated her words. But he knew what he saw by the river. A MacGregor killed Willa.

"Enough! We will speak of it no more until we have reached our home."

"You are all wrong, believe me. I ken my flesh and blood. Whoever murdered your sister canna be a MacGregor, and they canna be working on the will of Beiste."

Sorcha turned to Tyra with a pleading look. "Tyra, you have lived among us; you must ken this is not how my clan does things?"

Tyra just shook her head, opened her mouth as if to say something, then closed it and said no more.

That night Sorcha had a restless sleep. Much to her dismay, Bram insisted she sleep beside him so she would not run away. The only problem was, his idea of sleeping beside her meant he was curled around her. His front to her back, one arm over her waist and one leg atop hers. Her head tucked under his chin. And much to her annoyance, he slept like a log.

THE FOLLOWING MORNING, they set a fast pace again, and Sorcha remained bound and rode with Bram. She noticed Niall looked a lot paler. She wondered about the arrowhead still in his wound. Tyra was waiting until they reached their home. Then she would seek a better healer.

On the journey, Sorcha remained quiet and observed her surroundings. She also tried to reason with them again, to let her return home and sort out this mess, to no avail. Bram ensured she could not escape or leap off the horse by binding her feet as well.

"What will happen to me?" she asked.

"We will send demands to your kin for your release," Bram replied.

"Will your clan hurt me?" she asked.

"I will not let them," Bram replied without hesitation.

"Where will I stay?"

"You will remain with me until the laird is ready to take you. Then you will be his captive to do with as he pleases."

Sorcha shuddered at the thought of being handed over to another stranger.

The Gift

IT WAS THE THIRD NIGHT of their journey. Tyra slept close to Niall so she could check on his wound.

A few hours before dawn, a noise awakened Sorcha. She felt cold and knew that Bram no longer slept beside her. She saw him and Tyra hovering over Niall, who was feverish and pale. Sorcha knew if they did not get the fever down or clean the wound, he could die from it before they even reached their destination. Her sister-in-law Amelia was a gifted healer, and Sorcha had learned a lot from her.

Sorcha was not sure why she did it. If ever there was a moment to escape, it was now. But seeing Niall in agony and the worried looks on their faces affected her. So far, they had been kind to her, and if it was true that her clan had caused a major grievance against them, she could understand their motives.

Against her better judgment, Sorcha sat up and decided on a new approach.

"You need to remove the arrowhead from his flesh, or the wound will fester," she said.

They both looked at her, and Tyra said, "We need a healer with experience to do it. The barb is lodged deep."

Sorcha knew it was her niece Iona's arrowhead, crafted by Zala Fletcher, that was firmly lodged in Niall's thigh. That arrowhead would cause a great deal of damage on the way out. There was a way to remove it safely. Morag used a certain method, but Sorcha doubted they had the tool to do it, so she remained silent.

Another hour passed, and it was clear Niall's condition was rapidly deteriorating. Sorcha could feel the worry and tension in the room as Tyra and Bram carefully examined the wound again, trying to dislodge the arrowhead. She saw Niall descending into delirium, and she felt sympathy for his plight.

Then Bram turned to her and asked, "The Beast's wife is a healer, is she not?"

Sorcha nodded.

"Do you ken how to heal this wound long enough for us to get him home?"

"I have seen it done, but Morag is the one who kens how to do it."

Bram stilled and looked at her. Then he asked, "Morag, the old witch?"

"She is not a witch!" Sorcha hissed. "She is a healer with strange ways, and she can be annoying, but she is part of my family, and you will speak about her with respect."

"Alright, lass, I did not mean to offend. 'Tis just that Morag gave me something the last time I saw her."

Sorcha sat upright. "Morag gave you a package?"

"Aye."

"Show me!" Sorcha demanded. She knew Morag never gave a gift that did not have a purpose.

Bram went to his boist and pulled out an object wrapped in paper. "I dinnae ken what it is. But I could not bring myself to throw it away. Something about the way the old wit— I mean healer said, "twould mean the difference between life and death' made me reluctant to discard it."

He opened the wrapping, and Sorcha saw it was a diamond-shaped spoon. She stared in astonishment and said, "Bloody hell, Morag."

"What is it?" Bram asked.

"Do you want your brother to live?" Sorcha asked.

"Aye."

"Then untie me, and I will help you."

Both Tyra and Bram gave her a wary look. Then Niall screamed in pain and started mumbling incoherent words.

"I promise you I will not harm him. I only wish to help. If you will untie my hands and feet."

"Do it, Bram," Tyra said.

Bram nodded and released Sorcha. He then stood close by.

Sorcha got the pitcher of water and washed her hands. She then took the spoon from Bram. She made her way to the fire, poured scalding water over the utensil to keep it clean. She had watched Amelia clean things with boiling water before using them on her patients.

"What is it?" Bram asked.

"It is an arrowhead spoon. I must insert it into the wound to pull the barbs out," Sorcha replied.

Bram stared at the utensil, and it finally made sense. An arrowhead could fit inside the spoon's diamond-shaped cradle, and when pulled out, the barbs would sit within the spoon and not tear flesh. He knew then Sorcha spoke true and decided he could trust her to do it.

"Do you have whiskey?" she asked.

"Aye, why do you need it?"

"Tyra, pour some whiskey on the wound to clean it. Bram, you need to hold Niall down."

They both nodded.

Niall screamed in pain and started thrashing about, but Bram held him steady. Then they watched in awe as Sorcha inserted the spoon into Niall's wound and latched it to the arrowhead.

A few minutes later, the blood-soaked, barbed arrowhead lay on the table inside the spoon, and no flesh was damaged. Tyra was cleaning and stitching Niall's wound to place a bandage around it.

Bram was in awe. He had heard the MacGregor healers were highly skilled, but this was a different level again. Sorcha had kept her word, despite having no reason to save Niall. Bram wondered if maybe something did not quite add up.

Just before dawn, Niall's fever broke, and he slept peacefully. Bram knew if it were not for Sorcha and old Morag, Niall would have perished. He wondered, not for the first time, how the old woman knew exactly what he would need.

They remained a few more hours until Niall was well enough to ride, and that would give them all a chance to sleep. It was with some level of reluctance that Bram insisted Sorcha remain bound to him when they slept. She glared at him but then did as told.

The next day, Sorcha again pleaded her case, but Bram refused to hear her. He could not afford to deviate from his plan.

Sorcha refused to speak to any of them, and Bram knew if she was angry now, she would only grow angrier because he was about to do something that she would find unforgivable.

Sorcha broke her fast with Niall, who was sitting up. He looked better, although the fever had weakened him. He ate at a very slow pace.

"Thank you for saving my life. It would have been a shame if I had perished from a wound inflicted by a wee lass," he said.

Sorcha just smiled, thinking about how Iona had almost felled a fully grown warrior. Her niece would be so proud. "'Tis glad I am that you are well. But I wish you could talk your kin into letting me return home."

Niall looked sad and just shook his head. "I am sorry, lass, but 'tis not possible. Your clan started the unrest between us. This is the only way."

Sorcha just shook her head and ate her breakfast. It was a rustic but tasty gruel, and she needed all the energy she could get.

"Have you sent word to Beiste?" she asked Bram, who was sitting near the fireplace chewing on some dried meat while Tyra cooked more oatcakes for them to take on their journey.

Bram replied, "By sennight's end, my messenger in Glenorchy will deliver a missive to your brother stating our terms."

"You ken my family will not even look for me. I mean very little to them."

"Dinnae lie, Sorcha. You mean a great deal to them; otherwise, they would not have kept you close," Bram replied.

"What do you mean?" she asked.

"You should be in an abbey until you are wed, but we all ken women of your station are often unsafe in abbeys."

"So?" Sorcha asked, confused about the direction the conversation was headed.

"Your kin kept you with them where they could always protect you because you mean a lot more to your family than just a broodmare with a large dowry. And that makes you valuable to others."

Sorcha pondered Bram's words for some time and realized he was right. It would explain why she was constantly guarded. Her dowry was substantial, and anyone could force Beiste's hand if she were unprotected at the abbey. She realized the gravity of what her selfish actions had caused, and she became somber.

Sorcha had placed the MacGregors at risk because she had put her own needs above theirs. She knew her family would move heaven and earth to retrieve her, and that meant she had placed Beiste and her clan at the mercy of others.

She cursed herself for breaking the sacred rules her father had drummed into her as a child: *"The clan comes first, above all else. Protect the clan, protect your kin."* Sorcha had failed on all accounts and left them exposed. Her single act of defiance had left them vulnerable. For that, she could never forgive herself.

Sorcha washed down the gruel with some tea and contemplated Bram's words some more. She had to escape for the sake of her clan. Her hands and ankles remained bound, but she could find a sharp object on the journey to cut her ties.

Bram remained seated across the room. Sorcha wondered why he and Tyra kept glancing her way.

She ignored them and mentally planned her next escape. If only she did not feel so sleepy. Sorcha yawned; her eyelids grew heavy. She noticed Bram staring at her strangely before she realized her folly. *The bastards had drugged her again!*

Bram stood and strolled towards her. "I am sorry, love, but I canna risk you escaping us now," he said as he reached for her.

"I hate you!" Sorcha whispered before she passed out in his arms.

Chapter 3 – The MacGregors

MacGegor Keep, Glenorchy

"WHO THE DEVIL ARE THEY?" Beiste growled as he dismounted his destrier. "I want every single detail about the friends Sorcha kept and how she escaped the guardsmen."

They had pursued the culprits for miles, with no luck. It was as if they just vanished. It was a sure sign they were excellent horsemen because they covered their tracks well. Beiste knew whoever this Bram was, he had been planning this for some time.

Beiste cursed his ineptitude and lack of vigilance.

"Why did she not have guards on her?" Beiste asked Brodie.

"She had Lachlan."

Lachlan paled and stepped forward. "It was my failure to protect her, Chief. Something distracted me a moment and..." Lachlan's voice trailed off as he looked perturbed.

"And what?" Beiste demanded.

"I received a note for a meeting in the woods with a woman."

Beiste clenched his fists. "So, you left Sorcha unguarded because you thought of your pecker?"

"Aye, the woman was not there."

Beiste just shook his head and kept moving. "I want word sent far and wide requesting any knowledge of a man called 'Bram'. 'Tis not a common name; surely someone would have heard it mentioned."

"We will find them, brother; my men are gathering what news they can," Dalziel said as he walked beside Beiste.

Brodie clenched his jaw then said, "When I get my hands on Sorcha, I'm going to wallop her bahookie for hieing off with strangers!"

A feeling of failure descended upon the men that they had failed to protect their baby sister. They were still reeling that someone stole her right out from under their noses. If the Beast, the Bear, and the Wolf could not protect one lass, they had no hope.

"She has remained sheltered too long from the outside world. 'Twas not her fault they lured her away with promises of freedom," Arrowsmith said, bringing up the rear.

It was just near dusk, and the men had questioned everyone they knew who had contact with Sorcha in the last few days.

Beiste was now in a feral mood. If he discovered someone had sheltered the enemy intentionally within the village, he would kill them on the spot. He was about to return to his destrier when Lachlan approached again.

"Chieftain, I have news of the woman who lured Sorcha away."

"Go on."

Lachlan looked embarrassed, then replied, "Her name is Tyra, and she is from the Outer Hebrides. Although I suspect that is a lie she told others."

"How do you ken this?" Beiste asked.

Lachlan paused for a while then said, "She was the woman I was to meet that day, only she was not there." He blushed.

Beiste gritted his teeth, then said, "So she used her charms to lure you away from Sorcha?"

"Aye," Lachlan replied, guilt tinged his voice.

Beiste's eye twitched, then without warning, he threw a punch and Lachlan landed on the ground. "Get up!" Beiste seethed with rage. He was clenching his fists and ready to pummel Lachlan some more.

Brodie grabbed his shoulder. "Stand down, brother. You need to control your temper. None of this will help us find Sorcha any faster."

Lachlan stood to his full height with a split lip, and he looked contrite. "'Tis sorry I am, Chief. I will not rest until I find her. I swear it."

Beiste just looked away in disgust while Brodie gestured for Lachlan to leave.

It was then Dalziel arrived with an elderly man in tow. "Tell him what you told me," Dalziel said, and the man stepped forward.

"Chieftain MacGregor, I am an old tinker. I have traveled the length of Alba many a time, and I kenned the woman you are seeking. She said she was from the Hebrides, but I ken she is from Earra-Ghàidheal agus Bòd."

"How do you ken this?" Beiste asked.

"The thread of her plaid, 'tis blue and white with yellow stripes, the pigments of which are found in that region," the tinker replied.

"Thank you for your time," Beiste said and handed him some coin.

"What would someone from Argyll and Buit be wanting with Sorcha?" Arrowsmith asked.

"I dinnae ken, but we leave within the hour," Beiste said.

"Aye," Brodie and Dalziel agreed.

"No, you are not thinking clearly," Arrowsmith interjected. "None of you are."

"What do you mean?" Brodie asked.

Arrowsmith replied, "You canna ride to every place you hear she might be, or you will lose precious time. 'Tis best to send out men, especially Lachlan, to find more information on Tyra and Bram. Start at Argyll and Buit but dinnae limit the search there. These are both uncommon names, but we should be able to find which clan they hail from."

"Aye, you are right. I will send a missive to Dunsinane," Dalziel said.

"Why should we send Lachlan?" Brodie asked.

"Because he kens this Tyra woman well. He kens what she looks like, and if I'm not mistaken, he has a vested interest in finding her," Arrowsmith replied.

"Agreed." Dalziel nodded.

They realized then why Dalziel and Arrowsmith worked well together. They thought the same way. One was the king's assassin, the other the king's spy.

"Then what do we do in the meantime?" Beiste growled.

"We wait. They have taken her for a reason. They will reveal their plans and send us a message soon," Dalziel replied.

"But what if he hurts her and we can prevent it?" Beiste asked in a worried tone.

"A man who saves a bairn in a snowstorm will not harm Sorcha. No, Bram has been planning this for some time. He even sent a woman to get to her," Arrowsmith replied.

"Aye, he kens more about us than we do about him," Dalziel said.

"The question is, what have we done that would make him do such a thing?" Brodie asked before they mounted their horses and rode.

The Solar

WHEN THEY WERE BACK at the Keep, the mood was somber. Jonet, Sorcha's mother, wept for fear of her youngest child. Amelia, Zala, Clarissa, and Beth did what they could to settle the children and comfort Jonet. Even the children, who were usually boisterous, were quiet and sensed the loss of their aunt. They doubled guards over their watch, and they were not to wander off anywhere without an adult.

As they sat in Amelia's solar later that night, they discussed things as a family.

"Someone means to use Sorcha against us. We need to discover who would do such a thing," Zala said as she sat on Brodie's lap.

Amelia sat beside Beiste, and he gripped her hand as if it were a lifeline.

"I promised my da I would protect her, Amie. I promised I would always protect her since she was a bairn, and I have failed," Beiste said in a strangled voice tinged with worry.

Amelia offered him words of comfort. "Dinnae fash yourself, my love. Worry canna change a thing. We must keep a clear head and not become overwrought."

Beiste nodded and stared at the floor. Amelia pulled his head towards her. She framed his face with her hands and said, "You are Chieftain Beiste MacGregor, and you will find her. You have never let our clan down, Beiste, ever!"

Beiste stared into the steely eyes of the woman he loved, and not for the first time did he thank God that he had married her. Amelia believed in him and trusted him implicitly. He could never fail in her eyes. That humbled him. Beiste hauled Amelia onto his lap and just held her tight as she soothed him.

"There is usually one compelling reason for taking a woman captive, and that is to forge an alliance. Whoever this Bram is, he is not just anyone; he is a leader," Clarissa said as she sat on Dalziel's lap.

They nodded their heads.

"Do not worry about Sorcha. You have all trained her well. 'Tis this Bram person I feel sorry for, especially if she kicks him in the baw sack," Beth said, cuddled against Arrowsmith.

And for the first time since Sorcha disappeared, the group burst out laughing at the thought.

The Missive

SEVERAL DAYS LATER, a missive arrived for Beiste MacGregor. In it were accusations against them and terms he had to abide by to make amends.

Beiste roared with fury. Brodie, Dalziel, and Arrowsmith read the message and wondered what the bloody hell was going on. They had no dealings with the Hendersons of Glencoe in Argyll and Buit, let alone murdered any young lass. The only people they knew in Glencoe were the MacDonalds who were fighting against the Campbells, and they never involved themselves in the other clan battles.

"So, they kidnapped Sorcha as payback for us raiding their lands and murdering a Willa Henderson?" Dalziel scratched his head.

"Why the bloody hell would we raid their lands when we have plenty to eat and drink here?" Brodie pondered out loud.

Arrowsmith picked up the scrap of plaid that was enclosed with the message. "They found this bit of material on their land, and they blamed us?"

Their meeting was interrupted when a second missive arrived. This time it was from Lachlan. The message was brief. "I've found Sorcha. She is well, but things are not what they seem. You need to come and see for yourself."

The room went silent, then Beiste said, "'Tis time we paid a visit to these Hendersons of Glencoe."

Chapter 4 – A Captive

Bram's Longhouse, Glencoe

"WHAT HAVE YOU DONE, Bram Henderson?" his mother Fia wore a worried expression as Bram carried a sleeping Sorcha into the house. "Who is the lass and why are her hands bound?"

"'Tis the Beast's sister."

"Are ye daft?" his mother asked, wide-eyed and fearful. "You will bring the fire of the MacGregors upon us all!" She made the sign of the cross.

"Dinnae worry, Ma. I have a plan. I need to lay her down then I'll get Niall."

Fia was walking behind him. "Where will she sleep?"

"With me," Bram replied in a voice that brooked no opposition.

His mother glared at him. "I raised ye better than that, Bram Henderson. You'll not dally with the lass even if she is the enemy."

"*Haud yer wheesht*, Ma, I dinnae plan to bed her, just keep an eye on her. Niall is injured."

"What happened to Niall?"

"A wee bairn, a wee little lass shot him with an arrow. I tell you, Ma, the MacGregors breed them vicious! But he is all right; the Beast's sister saved his life."

Fia just shook her head. "I dinnae ken what the world is coming to."

"All is well as long as we keep her hidden lest Cruim finds out she's here before he needs to."

"What? You mean you haven't told the laird?" Fia screeched. "By the saints, I raised imbeciles! Lord help us all when Cruim discovers what you have done."

Bram placed Sorcha on his bed while his mother fussed about the room muttering to herself.

"Trust me, Ma, I ken what I am doing," Bram said before he went out to help Niall and Tyra.

Wee Little Faces

THE FOLLOWING MORNING, Sorcha woke to the sound of whispering children. For a moment, she thought she was back home in Glenorchy, surrounded by her nieces and nephews. But one look at the rafters, and she knew she was somewhere else entirely.

She rubbed her eyes and sat up quickly, only to be met with a wall of little faces peering up at her.

"Are you a faerie?" a little girl asked. She had curly black hair and thoughtful, light brown eyes.

"No, I am not a faerie. And who are you?" Sorcha asked.

"I am Mysie Henderson, and I am five summers old."

"Hello, Mysie, child of light," Sorcha said, for that was indeed the meaning of her name.

"Are you Uncle Bram's woman?" a young lad asked. He was about eight, and he stood scowling at her.

"No, I am not anyone's woman, and you are?"

"I am Domhnall Henderson," he replied with a puffed-up chest.

"So, you rule the world then, Domhnall?" Sorcha asked, referencing his name.

"Aye!"

"If you are not Uncle Bram's woman, why are you in his bed?" an older boy asked. He had a small sword at his waist, and his arms were folded across his chest.

Sorcha was still trying to think about how to respond when Mysie tugged at her dress.

"Aye, what is it Mysie?"

"Do you ken where Aunt Willa is? I miss her." The girl frowned.

Sorcha felt a strange pang in her chest. She was not about to tell her that Willa was dead. Instead, she said, "I am sorry but I dinnae ken where Willa is."

They were silent for a while, and then the door was thrown open, with Bram filling the doorway.

"Michael, what have I told ye about being in my room?" Bram said to the older boy.

Mysie ran to Bram with her arms open. He picked her up, kissed her cheek, and scolded the others as they tried to explain why they were there.

"Who is she, Uncle Bram?" the boys asked.

"She is none of your concern. Now out with all of you."

He placed Mysie outside the door and shooed the boys out.

When he closed the door he said to Sorcha, "Dinnae think to get the bairns to help you escape."

"I was not thinking anything. They came to me," Sorcha huffed.

"We will guard you every minute of the day so you canna harm any of my family in my absence."

Sorcha was outraged. "I would never hurt a bairn. You, on the other hand, are a different matter entirely." She glared, and Bram just frowned.

"I brought you a change of clothes. There is a privy outside and a stream nearby where you can wash. Iain, my cousin, will be here shortly to guard you, and Tyra will show you around. We dinnae live rich like your clan. I'll expect you to pull your weight with chores," Bram grumbled.

"You could always send me home if I am such a burden to you?" Sorcha replied defensively as she got off the bed.

Bram was silent as he observed her. He could not help but notice how bonnie Sorcha looked in the morning when she was piqued. He wondered what it would be like to wake up with her every morning. Bram mentally shook his head at the unwelcome thoughts and said, "You will remain here until the time is right." He moved towards the door.

"Until the time is right for what? Where are you going?" Sorcha asked.

"'Tis none of your concern, but trust me you will be safer in here than out there."

With that, Bram was gone, and Sorcha was left to navigate her way through this strange place. At least she knew one thing: they were Hendersons. She just needed to work out exactly where she was before she escaped.

Sorcha stepped out of her room and noticed it was a longhouse with flagstone floors and walls made of packed earth with dry stone. A fire burned in the center, and the high wooden rafters supported a thatched roof.

Down the other end of the building was a partitioned section where animals could sleep during the frosty nights. She surveyed the room; it was currently empty. It was rustic, but they kept it clean.

She took a few steps towards the fireplace when the main door opened, and a warrior greeted her. He bore the same family resemblance.

"So, you're the Beast's sister?" he asked.

"Aye," Sorcha replied.

He snorted after giving her a once over. "You're not as bonnie as Bram says you are. He must be half-blind. Come on then, dinnae stand aboot like deadwood. I have better things to do with my time."

He walked towards the door, and Sorcha grabbed her clothes and shuffled after him. She thought him a rude boar, but she was desperate to be outdoors.

"Are you Iain?" she asked.

"Aye," he replied, and ushered her ahead of him.

"Well, Iain, you are nowhere near as handsome as your cousin!" Sorcha snapped.

Iain paused for a moment in shock, but Sorcha stepped outside, leaving him behind.

It was then the most spectacular view of the Highlands greeted her. It took her breath away as she took it all in. They were in a glen and a river ran through it.

There was a long row of white houses side by side with the mountains beyond. The fields were lush with greenery. Cattle grazed in the pasture below, and the fragrant scent of wildflowers permeated the air. The sun broke through the clouds to reveal the bluest skies.

Iain passed her, so she ran to keep up.

Sorcha decided she was going to get as much information out of him as possible.

"Where are we?" she asked.

"In the Highlands," Iain replied.

"I ken that, but precisely where, in particular?"

"On Henderson land."

"And what is the closest town to here?"

"The one beyond the hills," he replied.

"Who lives in those cottages?" she asked.

"People," he muttered.

"Do you live in one of them?"

"I might," he said.

"Where does Tyra live?"

"The same place she has always lived," he replied.

Sorcha gritted her teeth and huffed under her breath. Getting any information out of Iain was like squeezing blood from a stone. She was too busy muttering at the ground to notice Iain smirking at her. When she looked up, his face was stoic and serious again.

They came to a wooded area where there was an outhouse and further down was a steady stream of clean water, which flowed from the mountains down into the river. Iain told her to freshen up, and he would remain on guard. He also warned her that if she tried to run, she would most likely get killed by his clan.

Sorcha hurried to take care of her needs. Then she quickly bathed in the river, scrubbing herself clean from head to toe with coarse lavender soap.

When she emerged, she felt invigorated and ready to take on the day.

Iain walked her back to the longhouse, where they ate a light meal, and waited for Tyra to instruct Sorcha on her daily chores.

When Tyra arrived, Sorcha was ready. She decided it was time to find out everything she could about this clan if she was ever going to escape.

Her first step was to make peace with the woman who had betrayed her.

Ex-Best Friend

TYRA WAS AWKWARD AROUND Sorcha. Gone was the easy rapport they once shared, replaced by guilt and open suspicion. Sorcha was doubly mistrustful, seeing as they had drugged her twice. But what hurt her the most was the mere fact that Tyra had used her. She had pretended to be her friend, and that meant she had pretended to like her, which stung.

Sorcha had grown up feeling the loneliness of being a child who could not speak. She rarely made friends, and when she did, they often found her behavior weird. She was not like other girls. Women her age gave her a wide berth, and men her age were too scared of her brothers to even become friendly towards her. But Tyra was different. She was the first person who took an interest in Sorcha, and to find out it was all a lie hurt her to her soul.

They walked a little while as Tyra showed Sorcha how to do various chores about the place. Sorcha merely inclined her head.

It was then Tyra broke the stalemate. "I'm sorry, Sorcha, but I had no choice."

"We always have a choice, Tyra," Sorcha replied.

"Maybe when you are a MacGregor, ye have choices, but us lesser mortals live by different rules," Tyra snapped.

"If I am to remain here for some time, tis best you dinnae pretend to be my friend," Sorcha bit out.

"I did not pretend; Sorcha, I genuinely like you as a friend."

"You have a funny way of showing it."

"Try to understand my side, Sorcha. Your clan killed my cousin Willa with no remorse. She was like a sister to me. Bram had to take action to make them stop."

"If you had only told me what was happening, I could have talked to Beiste. We might have seen a peaceful end to this."

"The world does not work that way, Sorcha. You have been sheltered too long."

"I guess we'll never ken now," Sorcha sighed.

Tyra turned her attention to her stitching, and they worked in silence.

"FUNNY, YOU DINNAE LOOK like a MacGregor," Fia said as she walked in through the door.

It surprised Sorcha to see an older woman entering. She had very striking features and high cheekbones. She held in her hand a basket of wool yarn.

"Is that good or bad?" Sorcha asked.

"Tis good, because the ones I have encountered around these parts are not verra pleasing to the eye."

Sorcha was not sure whether the woman was joking. She maintained a wry smile.

"I am Fia, Bram and Niall's ma, and Mysie, Domhnall and Michael are my oghaichean."

"Pleased to meet you," Sorcha replied, feeling nervous at the reception.

All she could say was, "Tis sorry I am for your loss, but you must believe me I had nothing to do with it."

Fia just sighed and replied, "Dinnae worry, lass, I ken it. Men wage war and women suffer for it. I am angry with your clan, but I doubt a young lass has much say in what her menfolk do."

"I dinnae think my clan had anything to do with Willa's death."

Fia stiffened and shook her head. "We always try to see the best in our kin. But sometimes they are not who we think they are."

Sorcha wanted to argue, but she would not take on a grieving mother looking to lay blame.

"Come then, you best learn to weave plaid. I am the clan seamstress, and I require deft fingers and good eyes for the task."

Sorcha agreed to help, hoping to garner more information from Fia.

It took a couple of hours to learn how to use the loom, but soon Sorcha was a dab hand at it, and with everything else in life, she absorbed the inner workings of most things like a sponge. For several hours she worked, losing herself in the repetitive patterns of her work.

This way it kept the homesickness at bay, and she could converse and gather more information.

What Sorcha could not extract from Iain, she discovered from Fia.

Mysie, Domhnall, and Michael were the children of Fia's late son. He was the laird until he fell ill and passed away. The lairdship shifted to a man named Cruim Henderson. Their family used to live in the Keep, but after the lairdship changed hands, they moved to the cottages.

Iain, Niall, Tyra, and Willa each had their own cottages, which were the white ones next door to the longhouse.

But the most important information of all was her location. Sorcha discovered she was in Glencoe, in Lochaber. They were Hendersons, and their closest neighbors were the MacDonalds.

Sorcha finally had more information to work with. All she needed now was a way to explore further afield, past the longhouse, and she also needed weapons. But she would work on that too.

And so it was that Sorcha fell into an easy routine. They filled her days with chores, and most mornings she would wake to find Mysie curled up in bed beside her. The children often followed her about, chatting about so many things. They reminded her of her nieces and nephews, whom she missed even more. Sorcha had always had an easy way with children, so she did not mind their curiosity. In the meantime, she gathered more information from them about the woods, the river, and different pathways leading in and out of Glencoe.

A guardsman watched Sorcha through the day while she went about doing chores. She helped Fia with the weaving in the afternoons, and she also helped Tyra prepare healing packs. It turned out the laird did not allow common folk access to the clan healer, so Tyra became their makeshift healer. Sorcha noted she was talented, but she knew Amelia could teach Tyra a lot more.

No one else came out to visit, and the family kept Sorcha hidden from the rest of their clan. They would venture into the village, but she remained a secret. She asked Niall and Iain when Bram would be back, and when she would meet the laird. Their response was always the same: "When the time is right."

The Return

THREE DAYS HAD PASSED, and Sorcha collapsed into bed, exhausted. She had thrown herself into her chores because it kept her mind occupied, and it also gave her more opportunities to gather information. She missed her clan so much. She swore if she ever got out of this predicament, she would never complain about being guarded ever again. She still had not ventured far from the glen because her guards were highly vigilant. But she had gleaned enough information to map a pathway to the next town following the River Coe.

Her best chance was to get to Loch Leven and make her way East from there. She could rummage for food—Amelia had taught her how—and Tyra had also returned Sorcha's bag and possessions. So, she at least had sturdy travel clothes and footwear to change into when she made her escape. She also had access to enough woolen plaids to keep her warm on the journey home. Sorcha crafted a crude bow and arrows out of wood, kindling, and bits of flax she found on her walks to the river. Zala had shown her how to make simple arrows by sharpening the ends of the twigs. The only thing Sorcha needed now was a sword or something more than a sgian-dubh. She dared not escape without one.

During the night, Sorcha felt the bed shift. She came alert and threw a punch at the large dark shadow.

"Ompf, stop it, tis me!" Bram said, pinning her arms to the bed.

"What are you doing here?" she demanded.

"Trying to sleep!" he growled.

"Then let me up so I can sleep elsewhere." She tried to push him off her, but Bram would not budge.

"I canna do that, love, or you might escape."

Before Sorcha could argue, Bram had her wrists tied, and he was curled around her so she faced him and slept in his arms.

Sorcha struggled to free herself, but he would not budge. He was too heavy to push away. She beat his chest with her bound fists and then gave up.

Bram chuckled, and she kicked his shin.

"Ouch!" she cried because it stubbed her toe. "I hate you, Bram Henderson!" she hissed.

"Aye, you've told me that before. Now go to sleep," he replied.

After much indignation and huffing and puffing, Sorcha fell asleep with her head tucked into Bram's neck, and it was the most restful night she had slept since her capture.

Bram pulled Sorcha tighter against him, kissed her forehead, and breathed in her lavender scent. He had to admit he had missed her. The whole time he was away, his thoughts often wandered to her.

It had taken longer than expected, but Bram had successfully negotiated a deal with the MacDonalds. Bram had fostered with the current laird, Ruadh MacDonald, and they trusted one another implicitly. Bram told him about Sorcha and the raids and that it was in their best interest as the closest neighbors to forge an alliance that did not include the Campbells. The MacDonalds agreed. With added numbers, Bram had the means to take on the MacGregors and right other wrongs. Finally, the time was right to make his move.

The woman in his arms was how he would kill two birds with one stone.

THE FOLLOWING MORNING, Bram awoke to an empty bed. Lying beside him was the rope he had used to tie Sorcha, but the woman in question was gone.

He shot straight up and out of bed, and two things came to him. The first was that Sorcha's bag, which he had tripped over when he came in last night, was missing, and the second, his broadsword, was gone.

"Damn it to hell!" he growled as he ran out into the main room.

His panic eased when he saw Iain watching over Sorcha and the bairns.

They were breaking their fast. Sorcha wore a plain brown tunic and the Henderson airisaidh. Her hair was tied back in a loose braid. She was seated at the table with his mother Fia, serving the children oatcakes with honey.

Mysie sat on her lap as Sorcha cooled her oatcake for her. Michael and Domhnall talked with their mouths full, telling her about their adventures, and even his brother and cousins grinned when Sorcha said something in return, and they all laughed.

Bram noticed it then. In his absence, his family was becoming attached to her. Even the children gravitated towards her. It was something his family did when Willa was alive. He gritted his teeth at the thought of Willa and struggled to reconcile his anger at the MacGregors, his grief for his sister, and his growing fondness for Sorcha.

But for the first time in months, the struggles they endured seemed a distant memory because of the enemy sitting at his table.

"Bram Henderson, will you put some clothes on!" his mother scolded, and they all turned to gawk at him.

Bram realized he was bare-chested, and his trews hung low over his hips.

He could not move because he caught something in Sorcha's eyes. She stared at his body and licked her lips. When her eyes locked with his, she blushed bright red that he had caught her.

Bram's mouth turned upwards into a grin. He felt exhilarated that his attraction to her was not one-sided.

"Aye, I was just looking for my sword," he said.

"'Tis above the mantle. I did not want the bairns to step on it," Sorcha replied.

He nodded, then retreated into his room, relieved that Sorcha was safe and under his roof.

Chapter 5 – In the Line of Fire

One Kiss

LATER THAT MORNING, Sorcha cornered Bram. "Have you heard anything from my kin?" she asked.

"Not yet, but I dinnae doubt they will be here soon."

"Twould save you a lot of trouble if you just let me go," she said.

"Dinnae worry, lass, when the time is right, I will let you leave."

"Your word on it?" She held out her hand for him to shake.

Bram clasped it and pulled her closer. "Aye, I give you my word, but it needs to be sealed with something else."

Sorcha looked confused. "What else is there?"

"One kiss."

Sorcha blushed, and her heart soared. She had never been kissed before. She had longed for her first kiss to be memorable. But was this man worthy of it?

"You are unsure?" Bram raised his brow.

"I have not been kissed before," she whispered.

Bram was stunned. He could not believe she had survived so long without.

"I was hoping to kiss a man at the village dance—"

Bram growled at the thought of any man enjoying her lips, and before Sorcha could finish her sentence, he lowered his head and claimed her first kiss.

When their lips touched, Bram felt it then. A powerful surge of emotion linking Sorcha to him. Sorcha gasped at first, then slowly opened her mouth as his tongue sought entry. Bram grunted and wrapped his arms around her, devouring her mouth and pulling her tighter against his chest.

Sorcha moaned with excitement. Finally, she had experienced her first kiss, and boy was it a grand feeling. She wound her arms around Bram's neck and stood on tiptoes to deepen the embrace.

They were locked in their intimate embrace when they were interrupted by Michael saying, "I told you she was his woman."

"Aye," Domhnall replied.

"Will she become our new ma?" Mysie asked.

"No, silly, she will become your aunt," Michael replied.

Sorcha and Bram immediately separated. Sorcha tried to straighten her clothing, and Bram cleared his throat. They were both panting for air.

"She's not my woman," Bram said.

"I'm not his woman," Sorcha said at the same time.

The children just looked confused.

"Now go on with your chores and mind your own matters," Bram said before walking off in one direction.

"I must go help your aunt Tyra," Sorcha said, blushing as she walked in the opposite direction, trying to straighten her hair.

BRAM CURSED HIMSELF. He was becoming far too attached to Sorcha MacGregor, and he needed to stick to his plan. There was no room in it to fall for his captive. He knew that is exactly what was happening to him. He was falling for the enemy, and that would ruin all his carefully laid plans.

Bram met with his men and informed them it was time.

SORCHA SENSED A CHANGE in Bram's attitude towards her since that one kiss. For the rest of the day, he was distant and colder, as if she had done something wrong. It hurt her but made her even more determined to escape. The man played havoc with her emotions, and she was tired of being kept in the dark.

That night when she had returned from the river after bathing, Bram stood outside his door.

Bram said, "You will stay in Willa's cottage from now on. A guard will keep watch over you. Tis best if you're kept separate from my family. You are my enemy and my captive, nothing more. Gather your belongings, Niall will walk you to the cottage."

Sorcha felt as if she had been slapped in the face. To think she gave that brute her first kiss. But she did not flinch or show any emotion. She stormed past Bram and gathered her things from the longhouse.

The entire family sat in silence watching her, and they glared at Bram, who ignored them all.

When she had gathered some things from the room and the kitchen, she moved towards the door.

"Tis an excellent decision. That way I too will remember my place, so when my brothers come to fetch me, I'll not feel any remorse when they thrash your hide!" she growled.

Sorcha made her way with Niall to Willa's cottage, her head held high. Once inside, she slammed the door, then grinned when she peered at her hand. She had swiped Bram's dagger and a small amount of valerian in the process.

All she needed was a sword and to retrieve her makeshift bow and arrow from the hollowed-out tree by the river. Then she was gone.

Sorcha had spent years being tutored by the best in ways of survival. And by the saints, she was going to use every one of her lessons to her advantage.

The Not-so-Great Escape

IT WAS EARLY THE NEXT morning, and Bram was returning to the longhouse after bathing in the river when he noticed something odd. Niall was supposed to be on guard, but he was not there. There was smoke rising from the chimney and some light, but something seemed off.

He knocked and there was no answer, so he knocked again, then pushed the door open and his blood boiled.

Niall was passed out against the wall, and his sword was missing. Sorcha was nowhere to be found.

He roused Niall awake. Bram was gripped with fear at what could happen to her. Not just by strangers or mercenaries in the forest, but if Cruim and his men got hold of her, she was good as dead.

Bram pounded on Iain's cottage door.

Iain answered and asked, "What is it?"

"Sorcha has escaped. We ride within the hour."

"Aye, I'll be there, cousin!" Iain replied.

"Iain, come back to bed, tis cold," a woman's voice called from inside the cottage. Iain looked embarrassed.

Bram gritted his teeth. "Tell me you have not taken up with her again."

Iain stared at the ground, and Bram just shook his head.

"You deserve better, cousin," Bram said, then ran back to the house.

When he entered the longhouse, he roused his mother. "Sorcha has escaped. We are going to find her."

Within minutes Bram, Iain, and Niall were riding out in search of Sorcha. They headed towards the village thinking she would seek help there, unaware she was headed in the opposite direction, taking the least traveled path.

SORCHA GRINNED AS SHE made her way keeping to the shadows and following along the river. She had hidden when Bram, Niall, and Iain rode off along the pathway above towards the village, no doubt in search of her. It would be some time before they realized she headed in the opposite direction.

She was weaving her way along the riverside, crunching on dead leaves and fern fronds when she heard movement ahead. Sorcha quickly ducked behind thick vegetation and hid. From her vantage point, she watched men run along the pathway from the woods. They headed to the longhouse. Sorcha was curious why they had their swords already drawn. But it was the words one of them spoke that chilled her to the marrow.

"'Tis three men, two women, and three bairns. We kill them all."

Sorcha knew they were talking about Bram's family. They did not know the men were away, which meant Tyra, Fia, and the bairns were going to be slaughtered.

She could not let that happen. It was her fault the men were not there to protect their kin. They may have taken her captive because of a misapprehension, but she did not wish ill upon the Hendersons. Sorcha took off in a sprint back towards the glen. She only hoped she made it in time to warn them and that she did not die.

Sorcha reached the homestead and remained hidden. The men had spread out, starting at the far end of the cottages. This gave her time. She knew the family would break their fast in the main house. She sprinted behind the longhouse and climbed in through the back window, startling them all.

"Sorcha, what the devil—"

"There are five men outside. They mean to kill you all. I came to warn you," she whispered.

Fia, Tyra, and the children instantly became alert.

Fia glanced out the window and moved fast. She ran to her room and emerged with two swords. She threw one at Tyra, who caught it by the handle.

Tyra ran to the wall and pulled down a targe. She threw it like a disc at Fia, who caught it. She then grabbed a second one from the wall.

Fia then addressed Michael, "You ken what you must do?"

"Aye," Michael nodded, grabbing Mysie and Domhnall by their hands. The three of them ran behind the partition to hide.

Tyra and Fia stood facing the doorway, their legs apart and swords and targe ready.

Sorcha stood between them, lifted her makeshift bow, nocked two arrows, and faced the doorway, waiting for the men to enter.

When the door was kicked open, the first two men through it met their deaths instantly, one with a makeshift arrow through his eye and the other with an arrow in the neck.

Sorcha heard the alarm and surprise in the voices of the three remaining. The element of surprise, something they had not expected. She nocked another two arrows and aimed at the doorway. She heard a noise to her left as a man broke through the side entryway. He ran straight at Fia. Fia turned and braced, blocking his sword with her targe. Then she hit back with her sword, which he blocked.

They were locked in combat and circling each other.

"The men are not here!" he yelled to the others outside, sounding triumphant that their odds of success were good against mere women. A second man entered the side building and charged straight at Tyra. She blocked him and was also engaged in combat.

Sorcha tried to hit both men with arrows, but the risk was too great, so she kept her eyes on a third man who yelled, "Find the bairns!"

To Sorcha's horror, she saw two more men approaching. This time, they had their shields up against her arrows.

Sorcha threw her bow down, grabbed Bram's dagger, which was strapped to her belt, and dropped to her knees as the third man ran at her swinging his sword.

She plunged the dagger deep into his belly and sliced across it.

He staggered, holding his stomach, and slumped backward, unable to move.

Sorcha heard a scream and watched as a blade sunk into Fia's shoulder. Her attacker withdrew it and was getting ready to strike the killing blow. Sorcha ran and leapt onto the attacker's back and stabbed him several times in the neck. He groaned in pain and fell to the ground.

Tyra had slain her assailant and was now locked in combat with another.

Sorcha glimpsed the children and was relieved to see them running into the woods.

"Sorcha! Protect my grandchildren. Keep them safe," Fia shouted before passing out.

"Go!" Tyra yelled as she used her targe to block the sword aiming for her head.

Sorcha jumped out the window and ran into the woods after the children. She feared there might be more men in the brushland. It was not long before she caught up to them, and Mysie ran towards her and wrapped her arms around her. "I am scared," Mysie whispered.

"'Tis normal to be scared when in danger, little one."

Michael and Domhnall stepped out of the woods also and ran to her.

Sorcha heard a sound close by as two men with swords drawn in the distance were running towards her. They were large, and she knew they would not be easy to fight.

"Listen to me," she said to the children. "You must run and stay hidden, you ken?"

They nodded.

"I will hold them off as long as I can, but you must survive, you hear me? And someday, tell my family that I love them."

Sorcha made sure the children had a head start. Then she gripped her sword, which she had stolen from Niall, and braced to take on her attackers.

One of the attackers scoffed at her as he drew closer, but Sorcha did not waiver as she stood her ground and held the sword steady. She just had to keep them distracted long enough for the children to escape.

He came running at her, and Sorcha sidestepped and managed a slicing cut to his arm. The other moved in and also received a swiping cut to the arm as Sorcha dodged his fist.

Sorcha knew that men often underestimated a woman's strength. She could use that to her advantage. Sorcha bent over, pretending she had been hit. Her assailant became cocky. He walked towards her and said, "This is why lassies should not fight. Your role is to rut and cook and that is all."

When he was still chortling, he got a shock when Sorcha stood and plunged her blade into his chest.

"This is why men should never assume women dinnae ken how to fight." She grabbed his sword out of his hand as he hit the ground, and now she held two swords.

"You bitch!" the other one yelled as he ran at her.

Sorcha braced and twirled both swords in her hand. She knew this was a fight to the death, but she was prepared. If this was how she was going to leave the world, at least it was doing a good deed.

As swords clashed, Sorcha moved fast, shifting her weight from one foot to the other and circling her opponent just as Zala had taught her. He was larger, but he was also heavy-footed. Sorcha could tire him out little by little.

"Come on, you big bastard! Is that all you can do?" she taunted, praying that the children were well away by now.

From the corner of her eye, she saw another two men emerge, but she kept on taunting them.

And that was how Bram, Niall, and Iain found Sorcha... standing in the forest, swords drawn, fighting like a warrior of old, while the children were scrambling to escape.

Sorcha MacGregor provided the only line of defense between the enemy and the Henderson children.

Bram felt a lump in his throat. She was fighting to the death to save his family. His only thought was that he was going to keep her. Her brothers be damned. Bram drew his sword, nudged his horse forward, and roared as he rode down the hillside.

Several minutes later, the attackers were dead, slain by the Henderson men and a MacGregor lass. One of them let it be known before he died, they were mercenaries hired by the laird.

Niall and Iain had retrieved the children, and Bram had his arms wrapped around Sorcha, refusing to let her go.

THAT NIGHT THE FAMILY gathered for a meal. Fia was wounded but otherwise alright. Tyra was also safe, and Bram's men had cleared the bodies and put the longhouse to rights.

Too exhausted to stay awake, Sorcha excused herself to go to bed early. The thought of escape was far from her mind now as she just wanted to sleep. She was just dozing when the door to her cottage opened, and Bram stepped through it. He closed the door and stood over her bed.

"Why did you not escape?" he asked.

"It was my fault you were not home, and I did not want your family to die because of me."

Bram just gazed at Sorcha with an intensity she had never seen before. Then he undid his sword belt and placed it on the table. He pulled his tunic off until he was bare-chested.

"What are you doing?" she asked.

"I am going to sleep, in here with you."

Sorcha opened her mouth to protest, then stopped because Bram's mouth was on hers and his body caged hers. His lips seared her skin as he kissed a path from her mouth down her neck as his hands roamed her body. She could feel his arousal prodding at the juncture between her thighs. They were both still clothed, but it felt positively sinful.

Bram reluctantly pulled away and wrapped her in his arms. They were both hot and flustered. "I do not ken what is happening between us, but from now on, you sleep with me, you ken?"

Sorcha nodded.

"Good," he said. Kissed her once more, then pulled her into his arms. "Sleep, love, tomorrow is a big day."

Chapter 6 – Power Shift

Henderson Keep, Glencoe

"BRAM, WHY HAVE YOU called this meeting?" Cruim asked, masking his surprise to see Bram and his family alive and well.

"We dinnae need an alliance with the Campbells," Bram said.

"Why not?" Cruim asked.

"Ruadh MacDonald has agreed to aid us instead, and I have something the MacGregor chieftain wants."

"What is that?" Cruim asked.

"Iain, bring her forward," Bram called out.

The crowd murmured, wondering what was afoot. It was then that Iain brought Sorcha into the hall.

"Who is she?" Cruim asked and squinted his eyes toward her.

"This is Sorcha MacGregor, Beiste MacGregor's sister. I took her captive to force his hand."

"Are you daft?" Cruim was red in the face. Bram also noticed several of Cruim's men seemed panic-stricken. Something was amiss.

Grant stepped forward and said, "Do you ken what you have done? You will kill us all!"

The murmuring became louder. Grant exchanged a glance with a man in the back of the room. Bram had seen him before. His name was Odart, and he was blonde-haired with a scar running across his right eyelid.

"How dare you do this behind my back!" Cruim shouted. "You have no right."

Bram did not move. Instead, he replied, "You are wrong. I have the authority to do it."

"Are you mounting a challenge for my position?" Cruim asked.

"Aye, I am. You are no longer fit to lead this clan."

Sorcha looked on in surprise. The room went silent.

Grant froze with his mouth agape in shock. "You canna take power from my da!" he yelled.

"I already have. Cruim Henderson, you tried to murder my entire family to prevent a challenge. Either step down as laird, or you will be physically removed, dead or alive."

The room erupted into rumblings.

"I did no such thing!" Cruim replied, but the crowd could tell he was lying.

Bram said, "From this moment, you are stripped of the right to lead and banished from Henderson land."

"You traitor! Kill him!" Cruim shouted at his men. But they dipped their heads and stared at the floor. "Grant, kill him!" he shouted at his son.

Grant read the room and realized his predicament. As the son of the old laird, he too could find himself banished. Grant took a step back and shook his head.

"You bloody coward!" Cruim hissed. He drew his sword and ran at Bram. The only problem was years of inactivity meant he was extremely unfit and unsteady on his feet. Before he could reach Bram, he tripped and fell off the dais, almost stabbing himself in the process.

Nobody moved. They just stared at him with utter contempt.

Cruim pushed himself up and surveyed the room. He realized then what he had not seen coming: Bram already had the support of the entire clan.

"You have a day to clear this building of your filth. Your women and children are welcome to remain, but you are not," Bram said.

Two clansmen stepped forward and ushered Cruim out of the room. He sputtered and raged and carried on, but everyone ignored him. Bram noticed Grant and Odart slipped out of the hall. He would be sure to keep an eye on them.

"I swear an oath of loyalty and pledge my sword to the new laird," Iain shouted and dropped to one knee with his hand at his chest.

"I swear an oath of loyalty and pledge my sword to the new laird," Niall shouted.

Soon every clansman in the Keep followed suit.

"What is happening?" Sorcha asked Tyra, who stood beside her.

"Bram is finally taking his rightful place as the new leader of Clan Henderson."

"What does that mean?" Sorcha asked.

"It means you now belong to me," Bram replied, his eyes boring into her soul.

He turned to address his clan and said, "As your new laird, I have allied with the MacDonalds. They will help us strike a deal with the MacGregors, who will arrive any day now. In the meantime, Sorcha MacGregor is under my protection because she is *mine*, and no one harms what belongs to me!"

"Aye," the room resounded in agreement.

As people moved toward Bram to offer their congratulations, Sorcha and Tyra stood to the side. "What happens to me now?" Sorcha whispered.

"Bram has claimed you publicly. That means you are under his protection until they reach an agreement with your kin."

"You ken that will ruin me, Tyra? I am an unwed woman, claimed by a man outside of wedlock," Sorcha hissed.

Tyra looked remorseful because she understood the ramification. "Aye, I am sorry, Sorcha. You are his now."

"Then I am already ruined." Sorcha felt a deep sadness settle in her bones. She would never find true love now. Even if she could return home, her reputation was in shreds. She vowed to make her escape, and this time nothing would induce her to return.

The New Laird

THE REMAINDER OF THE day, the laird's residence was a hive of activity as Bram ordered the entire building to be scrubbed clean, and he set about making changes. All hands were used as everyone joined in to work together.

Bram spent hours going over the ledgers and clan finances, and he was failing because nothing added up.

"Why dinnae you ask Sorcha to help you?" Michael asked when he saw Bram frowning over the paperwork.

"Why do you say that?"

"Because she can read, and she is verra good with sums. She has been teaching us to count."

"Has she now?" Bram raised a brow.

"Aye, even Mysie is learning to read."

"Is there anything the woman canna do?" Bram asked.

"I think you should marry her," Domhnall said. "She would make a pleasing wife. She cooks and fights with swords."

Bram almost spat out the water he was drinking. He coughed and replied, "I think you should go outside and help your uncle Niall with his tasks."

Meanwhile, Sorcha worked alongside the women. At first, some clanswomen were standoffish toward her, but Fia and Tyra made sure they intercepted any harsh words. They clarified that Sorcha was not the enemy, but her kin were, and until the situation was resolved, she would be treated fairly. Some still gave her wary glances, but when they saw she was a good worker, they left well enough alone.

Guards constantly flanked Sorcha, more for her own protection than anything else. Bram wanted nothing happening to her before her kin arrived. But to Sorcha, she felt stifled and restricted.

Let's Dance

THAT EVENING, THE FAMILY dressed in their finest garments and prepared for celebrations for the new laird at the Keep. Sorcha took a seat on the dais beside Tyra and Niall, while Bram sat with elders and important clansmen and their wives.

Sorcha watched the celebrations as several young women approached Bram to dance once the festivities began. A feeling of jealousy assailed her when one young woman wrapped her arms around him, and Bram grinned at her. She realized then that he was a laird, and he would no doubt marry a woman from a neighboring clan while Sorcha languished away with the stain on her reputation.

She watched as more young women threw themselves at Bram because now he held power, and he was a handsome man.

Soon Tyra was up and dancing, and Sorcha could not help but smile at her.

Tyra suddenly pulled Sorcha out of her chair. "Tis my fault you never made your first village dance. Let me make it up to you now!"

Sorcha was reluctant. "I really should not, Tyra, tis not my place—"

"Och, now who is this bonnie lass then?" A tall man with a ruddy complexion stood in front of Sorcha. He had dimpled cheeks, and his eyes sparkled when he smiled.

"I am Graham," he said. "May I have this dance?"

Sorcha looked over her shoulder and noticed Bram was still cavorting with the same woman, and then she thought, why not? She had never danced with a man before.

"Aye, I'd be happy to dance with you, Graham."

He grinned from ear to ear, grabbed her about the waist, and twirled her around as the music picked up the pace. Sorcha lost herself in the moment, threw her head back, and let loose. Soon she and Tyra were dancing with abandon, passed from one dance partner to the next as more young clansmen approached. In between jigs, Tyra and Sorcha sipped cider to cool themselves, then they were at it again.

"Tis me again!" Graham said as he completed the circle. "Would you care to sit awhile?" he asked.

"Aye, that would be nice. I fear I am worn out," Sorcha replied.

They both moved to a seat by the door for some cool air and chatted for a while before Graham asked, "Will you be taking part in 'The Chasing' tomorrow?"

"What is that?"

"Tis part of a tradition we have during the May-Day festival."

"What is involved?"

"Well, tis only for the single lads and lasses. It's a race to see which lass can make it the furthest without being caught by a man. If she reaches Loch Leven without being captured, then she can ask a boon of the laird, and he must grant it."

Sorcha's ears pricked up. He was describing a perfect escape plan.

"Really? This is a tradition, and it is honored?"

"Aye, I dinnae ken who started it. No doubt some randy men, but each year we all take part. Sometimes men compete for the same lass, which makes it harder for her to reach the Loch."

"What happens when you catch them?" she asked.

"We can claim a kiss or whatever else they wish to give." He raised his eyebrow with a wink, and Sorcha giggled.

"Sorcha!" Bram growled her name. He was standing behind her.

Graham immediately stood and said, "Laird."

Sorcha stood and replied, "Aye?"

"Tis time for bed," Bram said.

Sorcha blushed with embarrassment at being treated like a child. She also did not like what his words implied. Her back stiffened.

Bram was staring at her with a heated glare. Even Graham caught it and took a step back. But not before he said with a cheeky grin, "You'll think about it, Sorcha?"

Sorcha grinned. "Aye, I will."

"Then I best work on my running skills," Graham said before he beat a hasty retreat.

Bram clasped Sorcha's hand and practically dragged her back to the dais.

"What is he talking about?" he asked.

"'Tis nothing," Sorcha replied.

"Dinnae think to take up with any of my clansmen," Bram growled.

Sorcha rolled her eyes. "You canna stop me from taking up with whomever I please."

Bram glowered at her. "I can and I will. Remember, you are my captive and nothing more."

"How can I forget when you keep reminding me," Sorcha snapped, then refused to talk anymore.

BRAM WANTED TO KILL Graham. The man was far too handsome for his own good. When he saw him with Sorcha, he just saw red. Especially when Sorcha clearly enjoyed his company.

Bram had spent half the evening making polite conversation with vapid women when all he wanted to do was drag Sorcha away anytime he saw a young pup dancing with her. *The bastards!*

Not long after festivities wound down, Bram and his men were called away on urgent matters. Sorcha made her way back to Willa's cottage with Iain and Tyra, as she assumed that was where she was to sleep. Iain and Tyra were not living in the Keep with the others, and guardsmen were patrolling the glen now that Bram was their leader.

Sorcha bid goodnight to the others. She washed, changed, and got ready for bed.

During the night, she felt the bed shift again.

"Why are you sleeping here?" Bram asked.

"Why are you not at the Keep?" she replied.

"I sleep where you are. Tomorrow, you move into my chambers."

"No," Sorcha replied sleepily.

"We'll see," Bram replied before pulling her into his arms and resettling the blankets over them.

Sorcha was too tired to respond. She needed a good sleep because on the morrow, she was going to take part in The Chasing.

Chapter 7 – The Chasing

Henderson Land, Glencoe

BRAM STOOD ATOP THE hill, watching the festivities below. May Day celebrations were always a festive time for the clan. Now that Cruim was no longer the laird, there seemed to be a lighter atmosphere amongst the people.

Bram saw the men lining up for The Chasing and grinned. They were a rambunctious lot, and he chuckled at the friendly rivalry between competitors. As laird, he abstained from taking part this year. In the past, he had thoroughly enjoyed chasing down a bonnie woman for a kiss, but now he would just observe from the sidelines.

The unmarried women made their way to the starting line. There was much frivolity among them. The unattached men formed a line a short distance away to give the ladies a head start.

The rules were simple: men could capture a woman for a kiss. Any woman who escapes capture and grabs the marker from the loch is entitled to a boon. Whatever the request, the laird must grant it.

"I ken which one I'll be carrying away," Aldar, one chaser, said.

"I have my eye on the same lass," his friend Corey replied. "She's a bonnie one, light on her feet too."

"Ha! She is much too fast for your fat gut." Aldar chortled as they both howled with laughter and tried to push each other out of the way.

"Who are they talking about?" Bram asked Iain.

"Sorcha," Iain replied.

Bram's smile disappeared in an instant. He whipped his head to the starting line just in time to see Sorcha and Tyra arriving. Sorcha wore trews and a tunic. He knew then she was determined to outrun them all.

"No!" Bram shouted and clenched his fists. "She is a captive; she could use this to escape."

Iain smirked and replied, "Aye, I suppose she could. But dinnae worry, I'm sure Graham or any number of men down there will catch her first."

Bram whirled his head around to see Graham with one foot forward and his body bent low, ready to sprint. Bram remembered Sorcha's comments from the dance. Then he saw red. He stormed down the hillside and shouted to his cousin, "Tyra! Get gone, both of you!"

Tyra and Sorcha ignored him. They were focused on the man who held the carnyx close to his lips, ready to sound the starting signal.

Iain strode after Bram, trying to stop him. "Dinnae make a show, cousin, let them have their fun."

"Over my dead body!" Bram shouted.

It seemed forces were working against Bram because he was halfway down the hill when the carnyx sounded and the chase began.

Sorcha heard the horn blast and took off immediately in a hard sprint. She aimed to put as much distance between her and the pack. The stragglers would no doubt get caught first, lessening the number of competitors. It did not even occur to her that any man would chase her. Her sole purpose was to win the marker and claim a boon, her freedom.

What she was not expecting was several men making a beeline for her.

She heard one shout, "Och, I'm coming for ye, MacGregor!"

Sorcha ran faster, leaving him to eat the dust from her heels. She heard the crunching sound of feet crushing dead leaves as participants stomped and charged their way through the forest. Sorcha ran on, jumping over shrubs and vegetation and weaving and dodging chasers as she went.

"Sorcha! Tis me, Graham. Slow down."

She refused to turn her head but could see from the side of her eye Graham trying hard to keep pace with her. Men she had danced with the previous night also appeared in her periphery, but in their rivalry, they tripped over each other, landing in a heap.

She grinned and kept on running. Zigzagging her way through a copse of aspens, she heard Graham grumble before he disappeared and bowed out of contention.

But Sorcha would not relent. She had a boon to win, and for the first time, Sorcha realized she had a real chance of escape. Sorcha heard squeals and feminine giggles as one by one, chasers hauled women over their shoulders. It was then she hit her stride and began pacing at a more sustainable speed. She felt exhilarated and alive.

Soon the voices faded in the distance as chasers veered off to pursue easier prey. Then there was the quiet hum of the forest as the breeze swept through the trees and insects hovered over meandering dirt paths as the fragrant scent of flowers lingered in the air. Like a woodland creature, Sorcha ran on.

Soon she heard rushing water, and the closer she got, the sound grew louder until she could see cascading waterfalls in the distance. She knew she was close, and the anticipation of victory urged her on.

Then she saw it. Not too far in the distance, a solitary marker swayed in the breeze, marking the end of the race at the point where the river joined the loch. She knew that once she reached the clearing, she would win. There were no other people around, and she was close to freedom.

Sorcha had just leaped over a small shrub when she was startled by a sound to her right. She turned her head just in time to see Bram crashing through the forest, mowing down anything in his path, sprinting directly for her. Pure determination on his face. His muscles rippled as he ran with a fluid motion. His eyes fixed solely on her.

Sorcha let out a strangled cry as the adrenaline kicked in. She surged forward, trying to outrun him, but Bram closed the distance so fast she was scrambling to remain out of his reach.

She screamed, "Go away!"

He roared, "You're mine!"

Sorcha ran straight for a low-hanging tree branch, ducked, pulled it with her, then let it go. She heard a 'thwacking' sound, followed by cursing as the branch hit its mark.

She was mentally celebrating her victory, then shrieked in surprise when a muscular arm banded around her waist, hoisted her up in the air and over Bram's shoulder.

"Put me down, you brute!"

"Shut it, wench," he snarled as he kept running towards the waterfall.

The Rock Pool

THERE WAS AN ENTRANCE to the side which opened to a grotto, with rock pools hidden behind the cascading water. The morning sunlight reflected through the waterfall as flickering strobes of light danced around the cave wall.

Bram placed Sorcha on her feet and walked her backward against the rock-faced wall, caging her with his body. He was panting, his entire demeanor changed, and his eyes reflected hunger... hunger for her.

"No other man steals my kisses!" he growled as his mouth descended on hers, his tongue demanding entrance.

Sorcha gasped and opened up as their tongues intertwined. She felt completely at his mercy as she felt his hands move under her tunic, pushing the material upward until she felt his bare hands on her flesh.

Bram reluctantly pulled away and gazed at her with intensity. "I want you, Sorcha, and I'm going to have you."

"Aye, Bram," she murmured as she tried to catch her breath.

Bram grabbed the waistline of her trews and slid them down, urging her to remove her clothing. Within seconds, Sorcha stood naked before him, her voluptuous breasts a sumptuous feast for his blazing eyes.

Bram reluctantly pulled away from her to view his prize. "You're beautiful, *mo leannan*," he whispered reverently. He removed his leine and untied his trews with deft fingers, letting the garments fall to the floor. His hardened length sprang free and erect. Bram lifted Sorcha into his arms and waded into the rock pool until they were partly submerged. Then he lowered her in as he plunged beneath the surface. When they came up for air, he pulled her into his arms. They were face to face.

Bram stood with the water to his chest while Sorcha straddled his waist, her arms wound about his shoulders, her breasts bobbing just beneath the surface, the peaks stabbing against his chest, their mouths inches apart. Their bodies were wet with glistening water cascading down bare skin. He took Sorcha with a searing kiss. His hands gripped her buttocks, pulled her hard against him as his solid length caressed her inner folds beneath the surface. Bram thrust his hips, ensuring the tip of him bumped against her heated core, causing enough pressure to arouse her senses.

Sorcha moaned at the sensation and gripped Bram's shoulders tighter as she ground her hips against his length. Bram pulled away from her mouth and kissed a path down her neck to her breast. "Give me your nipple," he growled.

Sorcha obliged him and lifted her breast, bringing a stiffened peak to his hot, wet mouth. She moaned as the tip of Bram's tongue stabbed the tip several times before his mouth latched over her flesh and he suckled with force.

Sorcha felt as if a line of fire burned its way from her breast to her womb. She threw her head back and gasped for air. Her channel grew slick as Bram kept up the pressure. His breathing was ragged as he pushed harder against her pearl.

She heard a popping sound as Bram's mouth released its delicate morsel. "The other one," he snarled, "give it to me!" Sorcha obeyed as he laved it with his tongue, taking succor from her breast.

Sorcha felt a riot of emotions she had never experienced before. And she knew she would never be the same again. "Ahh... hmm..." she murmured incoherently as Bram lavished attention on her breast while building pressure between her thighs. She writhed against his palm, seeking a completion she was unsure about.

Bram groaned then walked them towards a small ledge at the shallow end of the pool, partly submerged. He was losing all sense of control. He sat her up on the ledge and lay her down, so she was on her back against the stone. Sorcha's hair hung over the sides, her pert breasts pointed straight up towards him as he stood over her, holding her thighs wide open. Her woman's core on display, a feast for his hungry eyes. Bram remained standing as the water reached his hips. The stone slab lay just beneath. It was the perfect height, bringing her heat in perfect alignment. Bram's hardened length jutted out, bobbing just beneath the surface, slapping against Sorcha's burning flesh.

"Look at me, Sorcha. I want you to ken who owns you," he whispered.

Sorcha gazed straight up into his heated eyes and licked her lips as she appreciated the aesthetics of his body. Her hands caressed his brawny arms. She felt positively wicked and alive. She wanted to explore his body in return, so she raised her head and licked his chest.

Bram gave out a strangled cry and eased her back down. "No, love, I will not last with your tongue on me. Another time." He chuckled when Sorcha pouted in return.

Bram pressed his thumb against her pearl and furiously rubbed her pleasure spot until Sorcha was riding his palm and squeezing her legs together. The sound of water slapping against flesh provided a rhythmic beat to their movements.

"That's it, love, aye, that's it. You're a beauty, lass, and you're mine," he said, urging her on.

Sorcha closed her eyes. Barely able to breathe, she gripped Bram's arms for purchase.

"Tell me you're mine!" he growled above her. His hand moving even faster.

"I'm yours," she shouted, so close to release.

"Then come for me and only me," he demanded.

With those words and the fury of his palm moving against her flesh, Sorcha came with a scream. She was still climaxing when Bram withdrew his hand and pulled her hips closer to the edge. With heavy lids, Sorcha gazed up at Bram just as his thickened ridge sought entrance.

"I need you, love. I'm sorry to take you here, but I need to claim you." His voice was a plea.

Sorcha looked down between them and spread her legs wider to accommodate him. She glimpsed his shaft, pushing its way into her glistening folds. She languidly gazed directly into his eyes. They were filled with something she had not seen before.

With one mighty surge, Bram thrust all the way inside her slickened sheath, driving home with a groan. Sorcha felt a pinch of pain before she engulfed his length and instantly detonated with another climax.

Bram shouted in ecstasy as the sensations of being inside Sorcha overwhelmed him. He gripped her hips and thrust into her heat repeatedly as he bent forward and licked her nipple. He felt like a conqueror as he pounded relentlessly into his captive while he stood hovering above her. Bram kept repeating, "You're mine, Sorcha, only mine."

Sorcha nodded and gripped his arms for purchase, fully submissive to his will. The sound of flesh slapping against flesh reverberated through the grotto. Hidden behind the waterfall from prying eyes, two lovers engaged in an intimate tryst.

Sorcha pushed up on her hips, seeking a deeper connection. She cried out, "Harder, Bram."

"Aye love, as you wish."

Bram pulled up her legs, placing the backs of her knees over his shoulders, and she was completely at his mercy. He leaned forward, placed his hands on the ledge, and thrust into her with greater force. The new position drove him deeper, and Sorcha was undone. She screamed as her inner core gripped him so hard, she shuddered with yet another fluttering release.

Bram swore, gritted his teeth. He could not hold off any longer. Then he threw his head back, drove in deep, and emptied his seed with a deafening roar. He came so hard his entire body was shaking as he jerked several times. His essence overflowed, coating their bodies.

Bram continued to glide his length in and out as he tried to catch his breath and slow the rapid beating of his heart. He released her legs and now lay above her, taking his weight with his elbows, slowly pumping in and out.

He leaned his head forward and kissed her deeply. Sorcha wound her arms about his neck and deepened the kiss. They remained intimate, connected as one. Lying on the rock ledge, they began a slow, sensual exploration as they fondled and caressed each other. Coming down off their physical high, they sought to deepen their emotional bond.

Bram had felt nothing like it before. The woman in his arms satisfied him to the core. He could not get enough of her. Bram felt himself hardening again, and Sorcha's breathing became erratic. Her eyes glazed over, and he knew she was preparing for another bout of coupling. He wondered how he had gotten so lucky. There was no way he was going to leave her unfulfilled as she writhed against his hips, seeking more.

Bram flipped their position while still connected, so she was now straddling him, and he was lying with his back against the ledge. "Ride me, love," he said as he stared up at her luscious breasts bouncing above his lips. He suckled a taut nipple and gripped her hips, nudging her into motion.

Sorcha proved a quick study and did as he commanded. Submissive to his demands, she rode Bram so hard he could barely breathe; he almost blacked out. He pulled her down and held her tight against him as he pounded into her with vigor. The sound of their bodies slapping against water created another layer of aural arousal. Soon they were soaring again into another earth-shattering climax. This time Sorcha's scream drowned out his shout as she collapsed, exhausted, on top of him.

It was an hour later, after they bathed and frolicked in the pool, that they emerged and dressed. Both of them laughing, stealing kisses, and caressing one another. Bram built a fire, and they sat beside it for warmth. He knew they had to head back soon, but he wanted to drag out their time together away from prying eyes for as long as possible. Sorcha rested her head on his shoulder, and he had her tucked into his side with an arm about her.

"I took your innocence today, love," he said. Seriousness marring his features.

"Aye," she replied.

"I did not take precautions."

Sorcha stilled, realizing what he meant. She had not even thought about the risk of pregnancy. "Dinnae think about anything beyond this moment," she said, too worried about the future to ruin their time together.

"Tis sorry I am. I had no right... you are still just my captive, and as laird, I am not at liberty to marry, but I—"

Sorcha's back instantly became rigid with the reminder she was just a captive. Nothing could come of this. Once her brothers sorted out this total mess, she would go home to Glenorchy and never return. Bram was making it clear to her, and she would be a fool if she entertained notions of love or any deeper feeling.

She cut him off. "Mayhap we should return to the Keep before your men look for you."

Sorcha pulled out of his embrace and prepared to leave.

Bram knew he had messed up. Sorcha was distant towards him as they walked back together. He tried to hold her hand, but she walked on ahead. He growled and grabbed it regardless, pulling her closer to him. "Dinnae be angry, lass, please."

Sorcha saw the regret in his eyes, and she nodded. She bit her lip to prevent words of affection from spilling out. She needed to remember that she was a mere pawn in a rivalry between clans.

Bram knew he had made his life a lot more complicated, especially when there was so much at stake with his clan. He needed time to think, but first, he would return Sorcha to the safety of the cottage, and then he would work out the rest.

When they emerged from the woods together, holding hands, partially wet and looking piqued, Bram noticed people smirking and grinning at them. His actions at The Chasing had revealed his hand, and there were no doubts people had pieced together enough to know how he and Sorcha had spent their time in the woods. His pursuit of Sorcha had indeed ruined her. There was much he needed to make right and much more he had to explain. He would cross that bridge when he came to it.

Discarded

IT WAS TWO DAYS SINCE the *Chasing*, and Sorcha had seen no sign of Bram. She continued with her chores and slept alone. The villagers smirked or grinned whenever she walked by. Bram had marked her as his mistress, and with his neglect, it would appear he was done with her already.

That stung, but she would not regret it. Their lovemaking at the rock pool was a memory she would carry with her for the rest of her days, even if it was just a mere tryst for him. She was even more determined to escape. She needed to return home, for she was homesick and heartsick as well.

Pleasurable Pursuits

THAT NIGHT, SORCHA remained in her cottage and did not attend the Keep for supper. She made herself a light repast, bathed, and prepared for bed.

She stoked the fire and settled in the chair, carving some arrows from the yew wood as she ruminated. It was closer to midnight when she had a small array of weapons.

Sorcha had just hidden them under the bed and was settling into sleep when she heard footsteps and murmuring outside. The door opened, and Bram stepped inside, closing it behind him.

He moved straight to the fire, where he began removing his cloak and then his clothing.

Sorcha sat up. "What are you doing here? Is something amiss in the supper hall?"

"Aye. You."

"Cease undressing," Sorcha scowled.

Bram simply dropped his plaid and stood before her, fully nude.

He stalked towards her and said, "I have missed you, and I canna breathe without you."

Before Sorcha could make head or tail of things, she was flat on her back, naked with Bram's tongue lodged deep inside her core. Her eyes rolled to the back of her head as she gripped the bedding. Not long afterward, Bram was above her when he exploded inside her welcome heat as she cried out with a shuddering release.

Several hours just before dawn, Bram was on his back on the bed, his legs apart as he schooled Sorcha in pleasures of the flesh. "Aye, love, that's it, it feels so good," he rasped. He gyrated his hips as Sorcha loved him with her mouth and tongue as her hand pumped his length. Bram could not take any more. He rose, flipped her onto her back, and drove home until they reached completion in each other's arms.

When Sorcha awoke the next morning, she was in bed alone but felt deliciously sore all over. The fire had been stoked. More wood was by the grate, and fresh milk, bread, and cheese were left on the table. She smiled at Bram's thoughtfulness, and her heart soared when she spotted the small bundle of fragrant wildflowers tied neatly together and placed beside her pillow. Whatever the future held, she would savor this memory forever.

Chapter 8

The Warning

SORCHA AND TYRA MADE their way to the Keep, joining the weaving circle. Equipped with their baskets of wool, they meandered along the footpath as it was a short walk to the glen. Usually, they chatted along the way, but Tyra had been quieter of late, as if something was bothering her.

"Are you well, Tyra?" Sorcha asked.

"Aye," she replied.

"Is something troubling you?"

There was a momentary pause before Tyra blurted out, "Sorcha, dinnae set your sights on Bram. I fear it will lead to a broken heart."

"I have done no such thing," Sorcha said defensively.

Tyra gave her a sympathetic look. "We all ken that he visits you often, and he has powerful feelings towards you, but it canna lead anywhere. Tis best you guard your heart. I tell you this as your friend. I dinnae want to see you hurt."

Sorcha blushed and nodded because Tyra was right. She would heed the warning. Bram was not his own man, and nothing more would ever come of their relationship.

Pretenders

WHEN THEY ARRIVED, the entire Keep was in a frenzy of activity. There was anticipation in the air.

"What is happening?" Sorcha asked when they joined the weaving circle.

The women gave each other furtive glances, and then Fia replied, "Tis the MacDonalds... they will be here on the morrow."

"So soon?" Tyra asked.

"Aye, Bram has been in meetings all morn," Fia replied.

"Why are the MacDonalds coming?" Sorcha asked out of curiosity. She had heard much about them from the children.

"The MacDonald laird wishes to introduce his sister Yesenda to Bram," Fia replied, giving Sorcha an awkward glance. Then Fia continued, "Yesenda has been away at the abbey. Her brother has gone to fetch her... now that she is of *marriageable* age."

It was then Sorcha understood, and she paled. She glanced over at Tyra and inwardly cursed herself for her naivety. Tyra and the other women were giving her pitying stares, and she knew why. Bram was betrothed to Yesenda MacDonald. It was an alliance that would ensure the Hendersons and MacDonalds united against her kin.

Sorcha gritted her teeth and clenched her fists. The thought that Bram would make love to her, then prepare to meet his future bride made her feel ill. Without the benefit or sanctity of marriage, she would become a pariah when the laird took a legal bride.

Suddenly the gravity of all her terrible choices weighed her down. Sorcha could not bear to remain in *Glencoe*, where she would have to witness Bram make a life with someone else. Marry someone else, raise their bairns while she remained as a captive, an outsider.

She wanted to scream out her frustrations to the world because she realized then she had fallen in love with her captor. She *loved* Bram, and the bastard was about to pledge his life to another woman. She needed to leave now. She needed to get away and leave this wretched place. She needed to go home.

Sorcha abruptly stood. "Please excuse me, I need to see to something." With that, she ran as fast as she could straight out of the Keep, and she did not stop. Tyra was hot on her heels.

Bram

BRAM STARED OUT THE window of his meeting room into the courtyard and observed the woman who had captured his heart. She was with the weavers, and he thought her the most beautiful creature he had ever seen. His memory of their couplings made him hard. She aroused in him not just physical pleasure but emotional satisfaction as well. He felt complete whenever she was near him. She was like a drug, and he was past the point of redemption.

His men sat around the table discussing alliance terms and contracts, and to Bram, they just became background noise as he homed in on Sorcha. It was not long before he noticed something was wrong. She looked stricken and hurt. His heart lurched when he saw her abruptly leave.

Without excusing himself, or second-guessing his decision, Bram bolted out the door, leaving his advisors confused at his abrupt exit.

SORCHA STORMED DOWN the dusty footpath. She felt humiliated. Bram had ruined her and toyed with her affections, and now she just needed to go home. She missed her family more than ever. Her one thought was to head to the cottage, retrieve her makeshift weapons, steal a horse, and rescue herself.

Her sadness turned to anger at her capture, and she could not wait for Beiste to arrive and kill everyone!

Tyra caught up to her. "Sorcha, come back! I am sorry you found out this way."

"Was Bram betrothed all this time?" she asked.

"I dinnae ken, Sorcha. I found out only yestereve, and I kenned you two were growing closer. I thought it best to warn you."

The sound of galloping horses interrupted them. On instinct, Sorcha grabbed Tyra and pulled her off the adjacent path and into the bushes.

Riders bearing the MacGregor plaid rode past. At first, Sorcha was elated to see her kin. She was about to shout out a greeting until she realized she did not recognize any of them. When they had passed, she remained hidden.

"Now do you believe us that your clan keeps raiding our land?" Tyra whispered.

"They may wear the colors, Tyra, but they are not MacGregors."

"Then who are they?" Tyra asked.

A voice close to Sorcha replied, "They are Campbells."

Sorcha almost jumped out of her skin as she whipped her head to the side to find Lachlan crouching nearby.

"Sorcha MacGregor, I have been searching for you everywhere," he said.

"Lachlan!" Sorcha whispered in surprise. She had never been so glad to see him.

She threw herself into his arms and burst into tears.

"Och, calm down, lass, tis alright." Lachlan hugged her in return, then got them both into a standing position.

Tyra stood to the side, watching the reunion and reeling from the knowledge that it was the Campbells who had been raiding their lands all this time.

Lachlan looked beyond Sorcha at Tyra, and all the warmth left his face. He gave her a cold, blank stare. The hatred burned from his eyes so much so, Tyra took a step back.

"Come, we best be going. Beiste and the others are a day away." Lachlan was already pulling Sorcha with him.

"No, we must tell Bram. It will change everything!" Tyra said, feeling panicked that they had made war with the MacGregors unnecessarily. "Where are you taking her?" she asked Lachlan.

"Home where she belongs. No thanks to your stinking clan," Lachlan replied, then spat on the ground. "Let's hope our paths never cross again because fair warning, Tyra, if I see you anywhere near Glenorchy, I'll make sure you live to regret it."

Tyra flinched and whispered, "Lachie..."

"Dinnae call me that!" He clenched his jaw and gave her a quelling look.

Tyra paled, then turned to plead with Sorcha. "Please, Sorcha, you canna leave. I am sorry for everything, but you must stay until Bram can make things right."

"Tyra, I have been a bird with clipped wings, mourning the loss of flight for too long. I want to go home. Please, let me go home," Sorcha replied. Sadness reflected in her eyes.

Lachlan clasped Sorcha's hand and pulled her away. Unfortunately, it was not soon enough.

"Remove your hands from my woman," Bram shouted as he walked into the clearing, his sword drawn, his men surrounding them.

Lachlan held tight to Sorcha and unsheathed his sword.

"Who the bloody hell are you?" Bram growled.

"I am Lachlan Gair, guardsman to chieftain Beiste MacGregor. You have done a grave injustice capturing Sorcha, and I mean to take her home." Lachlan kept Sorcha behind him.

The tension in the air increased.

Tyra stepped out in front of Lachlan to reason with Bram. "Dinnae hurt him, Bram, he speaks true. 'Tis a misundersta—aah!" Tyra shrieked when Lachlan grabbed her about the waist and hoisted her to the side.

"Dinnae ever place your body in harm's way to protect me!" he shouted at Tyra.

Tyra bit her lip, gazed at Lachlan, and whispered, "Sorry."

Lachlan just stared at Tyra's mouth and licked his lips. Both lost in some private exchange.

Sorcha looked between Tyra and Lachlan with confusion. She also noticed Bram glancing between them, his eyebrow raised.

"Your clansmen raided our lands and killed my sister," Bram shouted.

That seemed to grab Lachlan's attention. He replied, "The only clan raiding your lands as we speak is the Campbells! They may wear the colors, but they are not MacGregors. Someone has played you false."

Bram gripped the pommel of his sword. If Lachlan was correct, then he had made a grave error in judgment. Bram glanced at Tyra, and she nodded in agreement.

Iain stepped up beside him and said, "Cousin, there may be merit in what he claims. Grant was the one who insisted it was the MacGregors, and Cruim pushed that as the means for an alliance with the Campbells."

Bram paused then shouted to his men, "Find the raiders and bring them back alive."

He turned to Lachlan and said, "You will return to the Keep. There is much we need to discuss."

Lachlan gave him a wary look but then inclined his head.

"Sorcha, come to me," Bram said as he reached out his hand towards her.

Sorcha shook her head and clung to Lachlan.

"Sorcha! I said come to me, please." Bram glowered at her.

"With respect, Laird Henderson, I think you should prepare to meet Yesenda MacDonald," Sorcha snapped.

Bram flinched. He was hoping to speak to her privately on the matter but now was not the time. He dropped his hand and replied,

"Very well. But you will return to the Keep, and you will not leave without my permission." He signaled his guardsmen, and they surrounded them both as they all returned to the Keep.

News from Home

"TIS A FINE MESS YOU'VE got us into now, lass," Lachlan grumbled as he sat across from Sorcha.

They sat at a table in the main hall to take refreshments until the whole matter could be worked out. Lachlan was to be treated as a guest, and Sorcha was free to move about the Keep.

"How is everyone at home, Lachlan?" Sorcha asked.

"They are well but beside themselves with worry for you."

"And Beiste, is he truly angry with me?"

"I only ken that your brothers are going to whip your behind and most likely kill Bram once they arrive."

Sorcha paled. She worried for Bram. As annoying as this whole situation was, she did not want any harm to come to him. All she wanted was to leave and put this entire incident behind her. Yesenda MacDonald could deal with the big brute 'cause she was done with all the turmoil.

She was curious. "How did you find me, Lachlan?"

"It took some time. I followed a trail through Argyl and Bute, searching for a man named Bram and a woman named Tyra. It would appear both names were attached to this clan."

"How did you ken the raiders were Campbells?"

"I kenned something was amiss when people glanced at me oddly because of my plaid. Then I saw a tinker selling wares by the village. When I approached, he was fearful I would steal from him and said the MacGregors already took their fair share."

"Then what happened?"

"I figured someone was pretending to be us, and mayhap this set off the reason they captured you. It was not long before I saw some Campbells donning our plaid."

"So, have you been hiding all this time?"

"Aye, deep in the woods, biding my time, waiting for an opportunity to grab you."

"Do you think my brothers will wage war because of me?"

"Aye, they will."

"But these are good people, they have just been misguided. They have all treated me well despite my captivity."

"Has their laird treated you well, Sorcha?" Lachlan raised an eyebrow, and Sorcha blushed.

Lachlan gritted his teeth and said, "From the look on your face, I can tell he has done far more with you. You better believe it, Sorcha, your brothers are going to kill him."

Crofters Hut, Henderson Land

Midnight

"DAMN IT TO HELL!" BRAM yelled, picked up a chair, and smashed it over the fireplace. He then clenched his fists.

Grant Henderson, Cruim's eldest son, sat beaten and bloodied, tied to a chair alongside his friend Odart Campbell. They had captured both of them posing as MacGregors while raiding.

It was just as Lachlan had said. The entire raiding party was made up of Campbells and some of Cruim's followers. The whole thing was an elaborate ruse to force an alliance with the Campbells instead of the MacDonalds of Glencoe.

What they did not expect was Bram taking lairdship and ruining their plans.

Niall and Iain and several of Bram's men stared in disgust at the betrayers who had forced their hand.

Bram rubbed his forehead, a sinking feeling in his gut. He had done a terrible thing to an innocent bonnie woman. Captured her against her will, separated her from her family, refused to believe her when she pleaded for him to trust her. And now they would most likely go to war with Beiste MacGregor.

A scout arrived to inform him the MacGregors and MacDonalds would arrive in the morning. Bram frowned. He had grossly miscalculated and now had one hell of a situation on his hands. He knew there was only one path left open to him, and he was going to take it. All consequences be damned.

The MacDonalds

THE FOLLOWING MORNING, the MacDonalds arrived in great fanfare. The entire clan was present to welcome them, and Bram insisted Sorcha and Lachlan join them. They were all seated in the hall, sharing a light repast as Yesenda MacDonald, recently retrieved from Saddell Abbey in Argyl, met laird Bram Henderson for the first time since they were children.

Much to Sorcha's dismay, Yesenda MacDonald was a beauty. Worse yet, she had a lovely nature as well, which made hating her virtually impossible as far as Sorcha was concerned. Yesenda brought with her a substantial dowry that would help the Hendersons should the betrothal go ahead. Sorcha could not begrudge the alliance, and if it was any other woman, she would scratch her eyes out, but in this case, it would be like attacking a baby fawn.

With those maudlin thoughts, Sorcha refused to give Bram any of her attention, avoiding him like the plague.

When the men had retreated to a private chamber to discuss matters, it startled Sorcha to find Yesenda taking a seat beside her.

They sat in silence for some time until Yesenda said, "I see the way he looks at you."

"Who?"

"Bram."

"I dinnae ken what you mean," Sorcha replied.

"Do you not? Then mayhap you are the only one." Yesenda raised an eyebrow.

Sorcha blushed. "Bram is far too busy to bother with me."

"He looks at you with hunger. The type of look I hope to garner from a man of my choosing someday."

"What do you mean? You have no choice, Yesenda, and if you mean to cuckold Bram, you best think again!" Sorcha wondered why she was trying to protect the brute, but she could not help it.

"As much as I respect Bram, I dinnae want to marry him, and contrary to what most people think, including my brother, I have choices," Yesenda replied.

"Why are you telling me this?" Sorcha asked.

"Because I think we could come to an arrangement."

"What sort of arrangement?"

"I wanted out of that blasted abbey, so I agreed to this. It does not mean I intend to go through with it. Mayhap you could take my place?"

Sorcha looked at Yesenda as if she had lost her senses. "I think everyone would notice a difference."

"You are his lover, are you not?" Yesenda asked in her forthright manner.

"Aye. I mean no," Sorcha replied.

"You are not his lover?" Yesenda raised a questioning brow.

"No, I mean I am just a captive held here against my will."

"Are you a captive, Sorcha? Look around. You are not being treated like a prisoner, but part of the clan. If you played your cards better, you may secure your heart's desire."

"This is not my heart's desire, Yesenda. I want to marry a man who loves me and wants to raise bairns with me and occasionally shoot people with arrows."

Yesenda grinned. "And you think Bram is not that man?"

"I ken he is not. He all but confirmed he has no interest in a long-term arrangement with his captive."

Yesenda looked a little disappointed. "Very well then, tis no matter. I shall find some other way." She rose to leave.

Sorcha said, "Wait, why are you reluctant to wed?"

"We are all captives in one form or another, Sorcha. If I go through with this betrothal, it will destroy my clan. I do this to protect, not to harm."

Sorcha merely nodded and replied, "Then I wish you well, Yesenda."

"I wish you well also, Sorcha MacGregor. I daresay we shall meet again." With those cryptic words, Yesenda winked at her and returned to her seat.

Chapter 9 - The Reckoning

Dead Woman Walking

FOR THE REMAINDER OF the day, Bram was in talks with the MacDonalds, and Lachlan was invited to join them. In the meantime, Sorcha ventured to the waterfalls, where she could look out for her brothers. It was relatively easy to slip past the guards, as they were distracted by all the activity and movement within the Keep.

Sorcha had traveled a fair way. She had a sword and her old bow and arrows. She felt exhilarated and alive while she followed the line of the river. She paused when she heard footsteps approaching in the woods. She crouched down beside some thickets, waiting to see who it was. When she saw the one causing all the ruckus, she shook her head.

"Sorcha?" Mysie called out as she slid down the grassy embankment, searching for her.

"Mysie, what the devil are you doing here?" Sorcha asked, stepping out from her hiding place.

"I want to come with you," Mysie replied.

"What you need is to get your bahookie back to the Keep right now! 'Tis dangerous out here for a lass."

"But you're out here," she whined.

"'Tis different, I am a grown woman."

"Well, I want to be a grow'ded woman too."

Mysie stood in front of her with pleading big brown eyes. "Please? I willna be any trouble. I dinnae eat much, and I can walk fast. Everyone is too busy to play with me."

Sorcha sighed, then replied, "Very well, you may come with me."

When they had reached the clearing, Sorcha sat atop a boulder and pulled Mysie up to sit with her. From there, they could see for miles and keep a lookout for Sorcha's kin.

While they were chatting, she sensed someone watching them. Sorcha pulled Mysie to her side and nocked an arrow in her bow, pointing it into the greenery.

"Show yourself!" Sorcha yelled.

There was no answer, but she heard twigs cracking underfoot and the crunching sound of leaves. A young woman stepped out from behind a scraggly tree. She wore a long, plain brown tunic with a rustic brown coat that looked sewn together with rags. Her hair was long and unkempt, with bits of leaves strewn through it. She was also heavy with child and looked pale and weary.

Sorcha was about to ask if she needed help when Mysie shouted, "Aunt Willa!" and scrambled down the boulder before Sorcha could stop her.

Mysie had her arms wrapped around the woman's enormous belly. "I've missed you," Mysie said, with tears shimmering in her eyes.

The woman smiled and rubbed Mysie's hair. "I have missed you too, my bonnie one. Very much."

Sorcha jumped down and walked towards her.

"You are Willa? As in Willa Henderson?"

"Aye."

"Do you ken everyone believes you are dead?" Sorcha frowned.

"I am not dead, neither am I alive," Willa replied before she swayed on her feet.

Sorcha grabbed hold of her and helped her take a seat. Mysie looked on with concern.

"Mysie, gather some twigs and leaves for a fire? Dinnae go too far. Your aunt needs to get warm."

Mysie immediately went rummaging for kindling.

When she was out of earshot, Sorcha asked, "What happened, Willa?"

"A MacGregor did this to me," Willa said, as she stared blankly into the distance.

"Are you sure it was not someone pretending to be a MacGregor?"

"I am certain. He said he was a guardsman from Glenorchy. His name is Lachlan."

Sorcha was not sure how to proceed. She knew it could not be Lachlan, and someone had lied.

"And who are you? Why are you with my niece?" Willa asked.

"I am Sorcha MacGregor."

"Why are you here?" Willa bit out angrily.

"Your brother took me captive as vengeance for your death."

"Oh, he did?" Willa replied in shock.

"Aye, he did, and here you are alive and well," Sorcha snorted.

"If you are a captive, how come you are roaming free in the forest?" Willa asked.

"Because in the short time I've come to ken your brother, I've found him to be a dunce, and he does not even ken I'm here."

Willa stared at Sorcha a while, then burst out laughing. Her stomach was moving so much with her belly laugh, Sorcha panicked.

"Dinnae laugh, Willa, you might birth a bairn, and I dinnae ken how to deliver one." Sorcha glowered at her.

Willa just laughed harder. Then she grimaced in pain and clutched her belly.

"See! What did I just say?" Sorcha rubbed Willa's back, praying she did not go into labor.

"'Tis alright, it will pass," Willa said, and she took deep breaths.

"Willa, please come back to the Keep. Whoever this man is who hurt you, we can find him."

Willa choked back tears. "He did not hurt me. It was love. He loved me, but when he found out about the bairn, he said I was nothing to him. And he pushed me into the river."

Willa buried her face in her hands and sobbed.

Sorcha was at a loss about what to do. The woman before her was an emotional wreck. Laughing one minute, scowling the next, then crying.

"What happened after you fell in the river?" Sorcha asked softly.

"I wanted to die that day, and I could have swum to safety, but I sank beneath the rapids and hoped to drown. But somehow I survived."

"So, you have been hiding all this time? What were you planning to do, give birth in the forest? Have your baby delivered by birds?" Sorcha wore an incredulous expression.

Willa nodded, and the look on her face was forlorn and heartbroken.

Sorcha felt a strong affinity to her at that moment as she looked so young and reflected on her moroseness. Love was a powerful emotion, and when it is ripped away, it hurts.

"Oh, Willa, you canna be out here alone; you need your kin, your bairn needs your kin. They have mourned you all this time."

"How can I face them now? I am ruined. I lay with a man who was not my husband, and I have heaped shame upon my family." Willa wept.

Sorcha wanted to comfort her, but she knew she was in the same predicament. Love truly was an ass. Then she had a thought. "Willa, what if I told you, the only Lachlan from clan MacGregor is here now and in the Keep?"

"He is?" Willa sat up, surprised.

"Aye, do you want to confront him and tell Bram what happened?"

Willa clenched her jaw and replied, "I would like that. Because I want Bram to beat him to death!"

"That's the spirit!" Sorcha said.

Sorcha was just helping Willa to stand when the thunderous sound of galloping horses racing across compact earth rumbled through the forest. Sorcha stared across the landscape, and her heart sang because there in the distance she saw the most welcome sight she had ever seen. The real MacGregors had finally arrived, and leading the charge were Beiste, Brodie, and Dalziel.

"Sorcha, who are they?" Mysie asked in awe.

"Oh, Mysie, they are my brothers!" Sorcha replied, eyes glistening with tears.

Fight to the Death

WHEN THE MACGREGOR chieftain and his War Band of fifty rode into Glencoe, they struck fear into the hearts of those they passed. Their sheer size and menacing demeanor were enough to send people scurrying out of the way. Those who were brave enough to chance a closer look thought it odd that the legendary Beiste MacGregor carried a laughing Mysie Henderson on his lap. His second carried a heavily pregnant Willa Henderson, and Sorcha MacGregor rode behind his third.

Bram and the MacDonald laird waited at the front of the Keep to receive them, and Bram braced for the confrontation. It surprised him to see Sorcha and Mysie with the contingent, but it was not until he looked closely at the other woman that he froze, and the air left his lungs. He heard Iain and Niall and several other clansmen take a sharp intake of breath at the shock of seeing Willa Henderson very much alive.

Bram knew then he was doubly screwed. He wanted to greet Willa but refrained as the MacGregors dismounted.

Beiste placed Mysie gently on the ground and nudged her towards the women. Then he stormed over to Bram.

"Are you Bram Henderson?" Beiste shouted.

"Aye," Bram replied, extending his hand.

Before Bram could speak another word, Beiste planted his fist on his face.

Bram staggered backward, clutching his bleeding nose.

Hendersons and MacDonalds placed hands on their swords as the MacGregors spread out, forming a semicircle. The tension in the air was stifling.

Bram raised his hand to signal his men to remain calm. He tried to speak again when Beiste planted an uppercut to his jaw and a swift jab to his ribs. It caused Bram to stagger sideways, partly winded.

Laird Ruadh MacDonald stepped forward to intervene. He opened his mouth to speak until Beiste pointed his finger at him and roared, "You stay out of this, Ruadh!"

Ruadh shut his mouth, lifted his hands, palms facing out in surrender, and stepped back. He signaled to his men to do the same.

"Oh fuck," Bram groaned when he realized the MacGregors were a hell of a lot closer to the MacDonalds than he thought. There would be no help from that quarter.

"That's enough!" Sorcha yelled and marched straight through all the men, pushing some aside. She stood in front of Beiste and said, "Stop hitting him!"

"Get out of the way, Sorcha," Beiste shouted.

"Dinnae talk to her like that," Bram yelled as he instinctively pulled Sorcha behind him.

"Release my sister," Beiste bellowed.

"No, she's mine! I love her, and I'm going to marry her!" Bram bellowed in return.

The crowd grew quiet.

Sorcha looked shocked. Then her heart melted as she gazed lovingly into Bram's eyes and saw the same depth of feeling reflected at her.

Their intimate moment was ruined when Beiste roared, "Like hell you are!"

And then all hell broke loose.

Bram gently pushed Sorcha towards Ruadh MacDonald and said, "Watch her for me." Then he turned back to face her brother.

Beiste lunged for Bram, but this time Bram braced, sidestepped at the last minute, and punched Beiste in the jaw.

"I'm going to kill you, Henderson," Beiste said as he swung around, fully engaged and ready to beat Bram to a pulp.

"Ha! You can try, old man," Bram taunted.

"Who are you calling old, you muddy muc," Brodie said, glaring from the sidelines.

"Aye, you little shit," Dalziel piped in, staring dagger eyes at him.

"With respect, I'm referring to all three of you, old men," Bram smirked as if he had a death wish. He had his fists up in front of his face, and he was shifting on his feet from side to side.

That was all it took because in the next moment Bram was sidestepping and trying to defend himself against all three of Sorcha's brothers.

Niall and Iain waded into the melee to save him from himself, but Bram was not having it. He pushed them away.

"Stop this right now, or I will never speak to you again!" Sorcha screamed at her kin.

They ignored her.

Bram managed a swift uppercut to Brodie's jaw and planted a hard kick to Dalziel's side.

"'Tis alright *mo chridhe*, 'tis just like fighting toothless bairns," Bram yelled cockily before Beiste landed a knockout blow.

"Bram!" Sorcha screamed when he hit the ground. She ran and knelt beside him. She let out a heart-wrenching wail and burst into tears, thinking her brothers had killed him. She held Bram's head in her lap and kissed his cheeks. "Wake up, please wake up," she sobbed.

Beiste, Brodie, and Dalziel seemed confused at her reaction.

When Bram came to, he gingerly sat up and pulled Sorcha against his chest to soothe her. "'Tis alright, love, I am hale, dinnae cry." He hugged her tight and through his swollen lips he lisped, "Thee, thweeting I am better now, dinnae cry." He squinted at her through a swollen eye and a bloodied nose.

"You promise you are well?" Sorcha asked. "I could not bear it if something happened to you, Bram."

"Aye, love, I promith, I am hale." Bram carefully kissed her then and did not give one shit about her brothers hovering close by.

"Bloody hell," Beiste said.

"Fuck me," Dalziel added.

"Bollocks," Brodie grumbled.

All three of them grimaced at the realization their baby sister was in love with the stupid idiot. And by the fight Bram had just put up, it would appear the feeling was mutual.

Mysteries Solved

SEVERAL HOURS LATER, as order returned to the Keep and men nursed their bruises, all parties were made privy to the deceit that the previous Henderson laird and his family had perpetrated.

The MacGregors and the MacDonalds realized it was the Campbells who had a hand in Bram's misguided action to capture Sorcha, which helped appease them a little. Their mutual hatred of the Campbells meant the bulk of their anger was diverted to that clan and away from Bram.

It seemed only fitting that Bram marry Sorcha, not only because he clearly loved her and vice versa but because Bram let it slip that Sorcha could already carry his child.

"You will marry Sorcha as soon as possible or I'll kill you," Beiste threatened.

"Done, and I welcome it," Bram replied without hesitation.

Willa's reunion with her kin was nothing short of spectacular as the family welcomed her with open arms. Their months of grief and sorrow had turned to joy and hope for the future. They would also cherish her bairn, raising him as their own. The big mystery remained who had fathered her child.

When Willa attended the evening meal, she emerged from her chambers a different woman. Freshly bathed and dressed, she had eaten a succulent meal, and the color had returned to her cheeks. They had called her down to meet Lachlan so she could see for herself he was not the same man.

"Where is Lachlan?" Willa asked.

"He's right there, standing in front of you," Sorcha said as she pushed Lachlan in front of Willa.

Willa frowned. "That's not Lachlan."

"Aye, but this is the only Lachlan in our clan," Beiste replied.

"But that canna be. My Lachlan is tall with blonde hair, and he has a scar across his right eyelid."

"He has a what?" Bram asked.

"A scar across his right eyelid."

Bram looked at Iain and Niall, and they both closed their eyes in shock.

"Fucking hell!" Iain said.

"What is it?" Sorcha asked.

"Wait here."

Niall disappeared and returned later with Odart Campbell, who had paraded as a MacGregor during the raids.

"Is this him, Willa?" Bram asked.

"Aye, that's him. I take it he is not a MacGregor?" she frowned.

They all shook their heads.

"Then I suggest you beat him to a pulp!" Willa growled as Odart was led away pleading for mercy.

Cold Feet

"ARE YOU SURE YOU WANT to marry me?" Sorcha asked, a vulnerability in her eyes. "You were under some pressure when you agreed to it. I need you to ken you dinnae have to."

Bram stood facing her, his arms wound around her, their faces inches apart.

"I want it more than anything, minx. I had planned on it for a while, even when Yesenda was here. Ruadh and I had been trying to work out alliance terms with no marriage contracts when your brothers appeared."

"You were?"

"Aye. If only Beiste gave me a chance to explain myself, we could have worked something out with far less pain involved."

"What about Yesenda? Will she be all right?"

"Dinnae worry about Yesenda. She will be fine. 'Tis her brother Ruadh who will have his hands full now that she is out of the abbey."

"I just dinnae want you to regret this in the future. 'Tis why I think we should hold off another sennight in case you change your mind," Sorcha said.

"Never, love, ever. You will always be my captive, and I will always belong to you," Bram replied before sealing his vow with a kiss.

Chapter 10 – Weddings

MacGregor Land, Glenorchy Scotland - Captive

IT WAS A WEEK BEFORE her wedding, which Sorcha had insisted they postpone, making sure Bram was certain before he married her. She was getting jittery with cold feet and did not want to make any mistakes.

Sorcha had returned home to prepare for her wedding as the Hendersons would travel to Glenorchy for the nuptials. She desperately needed the love and support of her family for her big day, and she was sorely homesick to see the bairns and her family.

That morning, Amelia, Clarissa, Zala, and Beth, with all their children, invaded her chamber, insisting she bathe, style her hair, and try out her beautiful new chemise, kirtle, and surcoat. It was her wedding clothes their seamstress had fashioned especially for her.

It excited Sorcha to try the garments, so she did not complain overmuch. However, once she was dressed in all her attire, everyone disappeared without a trace.

She was just making her way down the flight of stairs to find out where everyone was when a gigantic shadow crossed into her line of vision.

"You're mine!" was all he said before Sorcha found a sack of cloth over her face, her hands bound, and he hoisted her over a broad shoulder. She tried to kick and struggled, trying to lash out. Then she heard a familiar voice.

"'Tis me, love, dinnae struggle. I've come to rescue you," Bram said.

She heard the whinny of a horse, and then she was seated on Bram's lap as they rode away.

When the sackcloth was removed, she glared at the most handsome face she had ever seen, then scowled when he just grinned at her like a fool.

"Sorry, *mo leannan*, but I canna wait another sennight to wed you, so I took matters into my own hands." Bram had placed her on the ground and untied her. He straightened her clothing and said, "You are truly beautiful, my love."

When Sorcha looked about her, they were at the rowan tree, and there was a large crowd of people forming a circle around it.

At the center was Abbot Hendry. He smiled at her.

"What are you about, Bram Henderson?" Sorcha asked.

He flung off his cloak, and underneath he wore his wedding tunic and Henderson plaid.

"Isn't it obvious, love? 'Tis our wedding day. We are getting married right now."

She whipped her head around and sure enough, there was her family, standing around the tree and her nieces and nephews, including Bram's family minus Willa, who had birthed a son and could not travel so soon.

"But we canna marry until next sennight."

"No, love, I refuse to wait any longer. I already lied to your brothers that we have been coupling often and 'tis not good to wait."

"Why on earth did you do tha—"

Bram moved in and covered her protests with his lips. Soon they were locked in an embrace that had them both breathless.

"Henderson, I suggest you marry my sister now before I beat you to death." Beiste glowered at Bram. Dalziel and Brodie scowled at him as well.

And with very little protest, Sorcha MacGregor married Bram Henderson under the rowan tree on MacGregor land, close to where he captured her. But as Bram would tell it to any who would listen, Sorcha had already captured his heart the moment she aimed her bow and arrow at his chest during a snowstorm.

The Newlyweds

BRAM AND SORCHA HAD been consummating their marriage vows since they left the wedding feast. Bram felt complete knowing that Sorcha was finally his in all ways, within the sanctity of marriage and the legalities of court. She was his to protect forever. Sorcha was content knowing that Bram was hers in all ways and there would be no others between them. Their union, formally recognized in all ways that mattered, gave them an added sense of love.

Sorcha was on her hands and knees, naked on their bed, while Bram was deep inside her and pounding her from behind. One hand fondled her plump breast, pinching the stiffened peak while the other rubbed her woman's pearl. Sorcha was repaying the gesture as her palm caressed him between her thighs. Her eyes momentarily rolled to the back of her head in pure bliss.

Bram had never experienced this level of satisfaction as he grunted with pleasure. He loved his wife and not for the first time wondered how lucky he was to have her.

"I can't hold on, Sorcha, I need to release..."

Sorcha contracted her inner walls harder as the sound of their bodies slapping together grew louder with each pounding thrust.

"Aargh..." Bram groaned as he stiffened and came. He rubbed her center harder, and Sorcha spasmed and screamed as her climax hit. Moments later they lay spent and replete, wrapped in each other's arms.

Bram's hand lovingly caressed Sorcha's belly. She was not showing yet, but he had a hunch about these things and told her so.

Sorcha placed a hand over Bram's and wondered, not for the first time, how she got so lucky being captured by her wild Highlander.

Worthy

IT WAS AFTER THE WEDDING festivities when the rest of the family was enjoying some quiet time in the hall around the fireplace. The newlyweds had retreated for the night while stragglers remained.

"We heard about what happened at Henderson Keep. Did you really thrash the poor lad in front of his clan?" Amelia asked the men.

"Aye," Beiste grunted, "but he fought back with no fear."

"Then he is very brave or very stupid," Zala replied.

"Sounds like a bit of both," Clarissa said.

"I kenned he was good for Sorcha the moment he pulled her behind him," Brodie said.

"Aye, I just wanted to see his reaction when threatened, and he did well," Dalziel replied.

"Och, but the son of a bitch riled my temper with his 'old man' remarks," Beiste chortled.

The men nodded and began chuckling while sipping their mead. "How about the 'toothless bairn' taunts?" Dalziel said, grinning. Then the three of them roared with laughter. They were quiet for a time, then burst out laughing again.

"Have you all gone mad? What has gotten into you three?" Amelia wondered.

"Bloody hell, woman, do you ken how long we have waited for a man courageous enough to take us on?" Beiste asked.

The women shook their heads.

"Forever! I was thinking we were going to have to let her marry some piss-weak horse's ass," Beiste grumbled.

Dalziel started laughing. "Remember when she was sixteen summers old, and that lad wanted to kiss her? I threatened him with a knife, and he damned near wet himself!"

They burst out laughing again.

"Or the young buck who ran at the sight of us and left Sorcha hanging upside down on the tree swing?" Brodie chortled. "I wanted to shake him for his stupidity. She could've broken her neck."

"And when I told the clansmen they'd be banished if they danced with her?" Beiste recalled, and they chuckled again.

"Aye, the bloody cowards stopped talking to her altogether," Dalziel said, shaking his head in disgust.

"Wait, so all this time you three have been setting up some sort of test for all these men?" Clarissa asked.

"Aye, and every single one of them failed except for that big dumb ox she just married." Beiste beamed with pride as if he had achieved something monumental.

"We figured it would take one hell of a man to manage her and stand up to us," Dalziel replied.

"He would have to love her enough to risk his own life, and that stupid oaf is exactly the type of man we approve of. He even stole her right out from under us, the bloody baw sack," Brodie said.

"Aye," all three of them grunted.

"He is exactly the type of fool we approve of," Beiste remarked.

The women just rolled their eyes and shook their heads.

"So, I take it you will do this with all our daughters?" Amelia asked.

"But of course, how else would we ken whether their men are worthy?" The three men looked at their wives as if they were daft.

Zala just shook her head and muttered, "Lord, help us all."

Epilogue

1048 Henderson Keep, Glencoe, Scotland

"SORCHA! HURRY, LOVE, or we'll be late. Your family is all still abed." Bram was impatiently hovering in the doorway of their chamber, trying to hurry his wife along.

"Wheesht, all right, I am coming. I dinnae ken why you are in such a rush."

Bram rolled his eyes as Sorcha tied her hair back. He tapped his foot impatiently as the seconds ticked by. Meanwhile, Sorcha took her time straightening her gown. She then picked a brooch and fastened it across her airisaidh. It looked as if she was reaching for something else when she yelped in surprise.

Bram was too impatient to wait, and he picked her up and carried her out of the room and down the stairs.

"Bram Henderson, put me down!"

"Shh, you take too long. We will miss all the fun."

He was carefully taking the stairs, as he did not want to drop her or harm their unborn babe. Sorcha clung to him, used to the daily ritual.

"What has come over you? I dinnae ken what is so important that we must break our fast so early. No one is around."

"Even more important that we are there," he replied.

When he reached the bottom and set her on her feet, he clasped her hand and dragged her behind him.

When they rounded the stairwell and came in view of the hall, that's when Sorcha saw it and realized why her husband was so impatient to get down to the hall.

Iona sat in the corner by the fireplace, talking to a young lad who looked keen on getting to know her better. They sat close together, holding hands.

Sorcha tugged on Bram's hand to stop him. "Bram Henderson, you will leave them alone and not embarrass her!"

"Like hell I will! We dinnae even ken who that lad is or what his intentions are."

"Bram," Sorcha hissed. "They are still young and just enjoying talking together."

"Just as I thought, he looks as if he is going to kiss her."

Bram was already across the room and bearing down on the two young lovers.

"Who are you?" he asked, scowling, with his arms folded and his feet spaced apart.

The two lovebirds were startled and instantly released their hands.

Sorcha could see the young lad was trembling with fear as Bram placed a hand on the pommel of his sword. The young boy paled.

"Uncle Bram, this is my good friend, Finn," Iona replied in a defiant tone.

"And does your friend have a tongue? Can he not speak for himself?" Bram asked while glaring at the young lad.

"I... I... uh..." Finn stammered and gulped.

"Well? Why are you sneaking about in the early hours of the morn?"

"I was not sneaking..."

"Aye, you were. What are your intentions towards my niece?" he boomed.

"Uncle Bram!" Iona stomped her foot.

And that's when it happened.

Finn paled and stepped behind Iona, pushing her forward as a shield.

Sorcha cringed because Finn just failed his first and only test. There would be no second chances.

A look of surprise crossed Iona's face at Finn's behavior, and she frowned.

Bram just sighed. Then said, "You are too young to be courting my niece, lad. Get on with you before Iona's da and uncles come down."

Finn nodded his head in relief and ran off without a single word or glance Iona's way.

"Blast it," Iona growled. She scowled at her uncle, then stormed off. It annoyed her that he had interfered, but she was more than annoyed that Finn had abandoned her without a word.

"Are you satisfied now? You big oaf." Sorcha shook her head.

Bram chuckled and replied, "She'll thank me someday."

"I canna see why. You scared away her beau and embarrassed her. Sometimes a girl just wants to ken a boy is interested even if it does not lead anywhere."

"He's not her beau. I heard him bragging yesterday that he would steal a kiss from the Beast's daughter. 'Tis best she is angry with me than have her heart broken by some worthless pup."

Sorcha just grinned at her husband. She stood on tiptoe and kissed him soundly on the lips.

"What was that for, love?" he asked as he pulled her closer.

"You're a good man, Bram Henderson, and a fine husband. And soon you will make a wonderful da."

"'Tis fortunate I am that I have married a wonderful woman too." He leaned down and gave her a searing kiss.

"Och, stop that now," Beiste grimaced and covered his eyes as he entered the hall, the rest of the family following behind. "'Tis enough to turn me off my food," he grumbled.

Sorcha and Bram just chuckled.

Purpose

THAT NIGHT, SORCHA looked about the hall as she sat on Bram's lap. She saw happy families around her, living and loving. She thanked the good Lord above that she had finally found her beloved Bram, and for the first time, she was thankful that she had people who guarded and protected her all her life.

Now she wished some of them could share in the same happiness. Mayhap she could help them find genuine love as well. Now that she was mistress of her own Keep, she could try to do some matchmaking of her own.

Starting with Lachlan. He sat quietly away from the others; he was broody and out of sorts, and she could see sadness there. He had been unlucky in love after shacking up on and off with Elora, who was engaged in a plot to kill Amelia. She was about to turn away from him when Tyra entered the hall, and that's when she saw it. Lachlan's eyes tracked Tyra, and he gritted his teeth when a warrior grabbed her and spun her around from behind. Lachlan growled and stood immediately, a hand on the pommel of this sword. Tyra blushed, then pushed the warrior away.

Kieran grabbed Lachlan's arm and yanked him back down.

What on earth was happening there?

She also wondered about Kieran. He deserved someone to love as well. There were rumors Kieran was courting someone, but he always denied it. She wondered why he would keep it quiet.

As Sorcha scanned the room, she saw more men in need of love and a kind woman.

She turned back to the dais, noting several single men around her. There was Niall, and Iain, who seemed to stare at Yesenda a fair bit. She also wondered about the MacDonald laird, Ruadh. He did not seem to be attached. She mentally counted others like Pier and Jean Luc from Northumbria and Torstein from Orkney.

Sorcha decided she had a higher calling. A higher purpose in life. She was going to make sure everyone around her found a love like hers. It was the least she could do. She also knew she could rely on her sisters to help her.

Her first target was Lachlan.

She took in a deep breath and turned to Tyra, who now sat beside her. "Tyra, can you do something for me?"

"Aye, anything cousin."

"I need you to help me plan a wedding."

"Whose wedding?"

"Lachlan's."

Tyra paled and looked over to where Lachlan was seated. She stammered, "I... I did not ken he was to marry."

"Aye, there is a woman who has captured his interest, and I want your help to make sure he receives a fine wedding feast."

"I... well, of course, if that is your wish... I hope they will be happy together. If you will excuse me, I forgot something." Tyra stood abruptly, looked as if she were about to vomit, and fled the hall.

A moment later, Sorcha watched Lachlan drag out his chair, stand, and stride out the same door Tyra had just disappeared through.

Sorcha smiled to herself.

"What are you grinning at?" Bram asked her as he brushed his lips against hers.

"I was just thinking how much I love my husband," she said as she wound her arms about his neck.

Bram replied, "'Tis a coincidence then because I was just thinking how much I love my wife."

The End

Lachlan & Tyra's story is up next...
https://elinaemerald.com/[1]
Sign up for Elina's Newsletter & Free Story
https://dl.bookfunnel.com/aiq0ubhpx6
Buy Direct & Save
https://payhip.com/elinaemerald

---

1. https://elinaemerald.com/books

Also by Elina Emerald

Cambridge
Lucas
Victor: Cambridge Book 2
Sebastian: Cambridge Book 3

FRIVEN EMPIRE
The Eleventh House: A Sci-fi Romance
The Vedora Key: A Sci-fi Romance
The Dead of Winter: A Sci-fi Romance

Keeper of Secrets
Highland Warrior: Keeper of Secrets
Highland Guard

Reformed Rogues
Betrothed to the Beast
Betrothed to the Beast
Handfasted to the Bear

Pledged to the Wolf

Reluctant Brides
Highlander Undone
His Runaway Bride
To Wed a Witch
To Have and to Hold
Your Money or Your Wife
Captive Hearts

The MacGregors
Arrowsmith
Sorcha
Lachlan

Standalone
Reformed Rogues plus Arrowsmith Book Bundle
To Tame a Viking Warlord

Watch for more at https://elinaemerald.com/books.